THE *Silence* BETWEEN *Heartbeats*

SHORT STORIES ON LOVE AND ALL THAT LINGERS AFTER

SHIRLEY SIATON

ISBN 978-1-961052-35-2 (hardcover)
ISBN 978-1-961052-34-5 (paperback)

1st Edition, October 2025

Published by Shirley S. Parabia
Cover by Lune Aesthete Book Designs
Interior formatting by Champagne Book Design

Inky Sword Book Publishing
Barangay Quezon, Arevalo, Iloilo City 5000
Republic of the Philippines
inkysword.com

A NOTE FOR THE READER

These stories were written for the tender-hearted. For those who have loved deeply, lost quietly, and kept going anyway.

Inside, you'll find bittersweet moments, quiet heartbreaks, and the kind of love that lingers even after goodbye. Some stories touch on grief, illness, longing, loneliness, and the ache of things left unsaid.

There is no explicit content in these pages, but the emotional themes are best suited for readers aged 16 and above.

Please read gently. And when it hurts, pause. Breathe. Come back only when you're ready.

You are not alone. 🖤

To Yono

You made me believe
That stories are not promises
Neither are they guarantees

You made me believe
That stories are infinite possibilities
And reasons to keep going
And hoping

So let's keep going
Story by story
Page by page
Hope by hope

CONTENTS

THE *Silence* BETWEEN *Heartbeats*

THE
SILENCE
BETWEEN
HEARTBEATS

I used to think forgetting was like thunder
Echoing, decisive, loud
A final, shrieking split of the sky

But now I know the truth
The deepest memories don't scream
They don't even fight
They don't even cry

They simply stay
Quietly, gently, softly
A breath in the pause before the next
A hush between heartbeats

That's where you now live
Not in photographs
Not in old, yellowed letters
Or messages saved from phone to phone
Not in the places we once stood
Not even in the ghost of touches and almosts

You live in the spaces no one else can reach
You return when I am still
When the world stops spinning just long enough
For silence to find me

You remain in the quiet we once shared
You are remembered in the warm breeze
When my chest rises and falls
With the rhythm of living

And there
In the pauses between
I feel you
I see you
Once more

It's not pain
It's not even longing
Not anymore
It's just you
A secret I never told anyone
A truth my heart never let go of

Some are remembered in words
You are remembered in stillness
And I don't think I will ever stop
Hearing you there

In the silence

In the pauses

The in-between

Of my heartbeats

CHAPTER 1

The Train that Didn't Stop

I MEET HIM ON THE WORST DAY OF MY LIFE.

The air is sticky with summer heat, the kind that clings to my skin and makes everything feel heavier than it is. I have just quit my job at the BPO. My apartment lease has ended. My father, who has already forgotten my name, has finally forgotten my face.

And the train is late.

I sit on the steel bench of the platform with my suitcase between my feet and a knot behind my ribs, wondering if it's too dramatic to just cry in public.

He sits two benches down, headphones in, tapping a pencil against a worn, leather-bound notebook.

I don't notice him at first. He is too quiet, too still—a shadow that has forgotten it isn't supposed to be noticed. But then he looks up, and our eyes meet, and something inside me trips.

He smiles like I'm a secret he already knows.

I look away.

Ten minutes later, he walks over and offers me a slightly squished sandwich in a plastic container.

"I'm not hungry," I say, even though I haven't eaten since yesterday evening.

He shrugs and places it beside me anyway, then takes a seat.

"The food in the station sucks. I got this sandwich from a vendor I've known since I was five. So this one's not poisoned. Probably."

I don't remember why I laugh, only that I do. And it's the first time something doesn't hurt in days.

His name is Leon.

He is a sketch artist. He draws strangers on trains and leaves the portraits behind—between pages of abandoned books, folded inside vending machine slots, under empty coffee cups. He says he likes the idea of someone finding a version of themselves they don't know exists.

"Why do you leave them?" I ask.

"Because art shouldn't beg to be kept."

He never asks where I'm going.

I never ask where he's from.

There's a kind of reverence in our silence, the way two people can exist next to each other without taking apart the ache they carry. He doesn't pry into my sorrow. I don't poke at his shadows. We just…sit there.

When the train finally comes, we board together.

He helps me hoist my suitcase into the overhead rack, then settles across from me. Not beside, but across. As if even now, he knows distance is safer.

He draws for two hours straight while I stare out the window pretending not to look at him.

When I finally doze off, he places a folded piece of paper in my lap.

It is me.

But not the broken, hollow me I see in mirrors. This girl is still bent, yes, but blooming anyway. Wind in her hair, scratches on her arms, fire in her eyes.

When I wake, he is gone.

It takes almost a year before I see him again.

He is standing in a bookstore, at a mall near the station, holding a cup of coffee and arguing with a child about whether unicorns can fly.

(They can't, he posits. They don't even exist. The child insists they do, and they most definitely *can*.)

I stand there too long, holding a book I'm not reading, watching him laugh like nothing has changed.

He looks up.

And again, he smiles like he already knows me.

"You forgot your sandwich," he says, as if a year hasn't happened.

"You ran off the train."

"You snored."

"I did not."

"You did."

He buys me the same drink as his. We sit on the coffee shop's wooden stools and watch people rushing around us.

The mall's crowded, but I feel still. Almost at peace.

He doesn't ask where I've been. I don't ask why he disappeared.

But when I reach into my bag that night, I find a sketch folded between my umbrella and tiny portable fan.

This time, it's both of us. On a train that never arrives. Sitting across from each other. Still not touching.

He texts me. We meet again. And again.

At the same coffee shop near the bookstore.

We become something close to almost.

Not quite friends. Not quite lovers. Always somewhere between.

He calls when the sky is the color of regret. I answer when my bones feel too hollow.

We walk, or sit, or breathe together in alleys and parks and bookstores way past closing time.

We haunt tables in the shadows of all-hours convenience stores, eating cup noodles like a ritual. Chicken for him, beef for me.

He drops me off at my boardinghouse on his rent-to-own motorcycle.

Once, I ask if he believes in fate.

He says, "Only when it's too late."

I fall in love with him in moments.

When he saves a moth from a coffee shop window and tells it, gently, "Not today."

When he cries watching a rerun of a movie where a pack of sled dogs gets left behind.

When he touches my wrist like he's afraid of breaking the air between us.

But Leon is like fog.

He arrives when I'm not looking and leaves before I can hold on.

One time, he tells me, softly, "Some people are just stopovers, not destinations."

I nod as if I agree. Or at least understand.

But I'm already building a home at the station of my heart.

The night he tells me goodbye, it doesn't rain.

It should, I think.

We sit at the same platform where we first meet, now strangers all over again.

"I got accepted," he says.

"To what?"

"A Fine Arts scholarship. You know, at the university. In the city."

My throat closes around the word *stay*, so I smile instead.

"Wow, that's awesome. Congratulations."

He reaches into his bag and hands me a notebook. The same old leather one he always carries.

I undo the silver magnetic button.

Inside are sketches.

Me, again and again.

Me laughing. Me angry. Me walking away. Me staring out a train window, always alone.

"I don't know why it's always you, Jen," he tells me quietly.

"I do," I answer, just as softly.

He smiles his knowing smile, one last time.

"Of course you do."

He kisses my forehead, stands, and walks onto the train.

I don't follow.

He doesn't look back.

I still take the train sometimes.

I sit on the platform and wait for a shadow to sit two benches down and offer me a sandwich.

It never happens.

But sometimes, when the sky is the color of regret and the wind tastes like a name you haven't said in years, I pull out his sketches and hold them close to my chest.

I still don't know if Leon is real.

Maybe he is a dream dressed in skin.

Maybe he is just another train I never board.

But I hope—god, I hope—somewhere in the big city, there's a drawing of me.

Smiling. Standing. Finally whole.

Maybe, in that version, I get on the train.

Maybe, in that version, he stays.

Maybe.

Always maybe.

CHAPTER 2

Bruise-Colored Love

I SWEAR I WILL NEVER FALL FOR SOMEONE LIKE HIM.

I repeat it every morning like prayer, or superstition.

Or a spell I can clench between my teeth so I don't swallow it by accident.

And then he leans in the doorway of the student council room, one cheek bruised, mouth cut at the corner, smirk set to devastation levels, and my pulse does the exact opposite of prayer.

It races.

And it gives in to temptation.

The silence between heartbeats opens—small and bright, a beautiful and dangerous trap—and I walk into it.

"Move," I say, arms full of folders, hair pinned into the version of me adults trust.

"What's the magic word, princess?" he asks, not budging an inch.

"Please don't make me staple your mouth shut before the outreach drive," I say. "I need both hands to collect all the donations I could."

He lifts both palms, laughing. "Donations. Be still, my heart."

"It would be a public service to the inner city villages." I shoulder past him and place the folders on the table with a resounding *thunk.* "Did you finish painting the backdrop?"

"Two coats," he says. "Three if you count the one on my lungs."

"You're not supposed to paint in a closed room."

"You're not supposed to micromanage a guy who volunteered on his day off." He leans into my space, that lazy grin I hate, the citrus-ash scent I hate more. "But here we are."

"Here we are," I echo, rolling my eyes.

Outside, the auditorium speakers hiccup with feedback. Inside, the room's fan ticks like a tired metronome. I circle items on the checklist so hard the pen almost tears the paper.

He watches me. He always watches me, as if I'm a language he only half understands but wants to speak without an accent.

"Tell me again why you're here," I say. "And don't even try to lie."

"Because the guidance counselor said 'service hours,'" he says. "And because you asked nicely."

"I didn't ask," I lie.

I did ask for him. Not by name, but by skill.

I knew he was the only one who could paint the backdrop for the fundraiser show without batting an eye.

He tips his head. "You didn't have to. Who else could put up with me?"

I hate the way that lands. I hate the way my chest answers with a soft, traitorous ache.

"Do you ever," I ask, still looking at my checklist, "get tired of being a problem?"

"Do you ever," he fires back, "get tired of putting up with problems that can't be solved?"

We hold each other's eyes like that. Whatever is between us feels it's stretched too tight.

Around us, the room hums and thrums. The hallway fills and empties with bodies and noise. Between us, the unsaid is a knife we both press a little too close to our throats.

Then I clear mine. "If the backdrop peels, I'll personally haunt you."

"Hot," he says, and saunters out before I can scold him for existing.

I look at the space where he stood a second too long, and turn away.

He shows up again two nights later at the university gates, leaning against the hood of his gray car, jaw blooming purple, knuckles skinned almost raw.

"What happened?" The words slip out before I can stop them. "Didn't see you in class yesterday."

"What do you think?" he says, grinning.

"You're such an idiot."

"And you're such a saint. Wanna heal me?"

"I don't fix broken things," I say automatically.

But my hand is already reaching up, thumb hovering over the bruise. I'm close enough to see the flecks of gold in his otherwise dark brown eyes. Close enough to see the new crack in his bottom lip where the skin should be soft.

He catches my wrist and holds it there. Not hard, but just enough to make my pulse jump against his fingers.

"See?" he rasps. "You already do."

"Let go," I say.

He does. Immediately. The way he obeys makes my stomach drop. I hate him more for that than for the smirk.

"Get in," he says, tilting his chin at the passenger door.

"Now?"

"Unless you're busy scheduling your next attempt at saving the world. You should try living normally like the rest of us, princess. Who knows, you might like it."

I frown at him, ready to bite back.

But I hesitate.

The look in his eyes says everything his lips couldn't.

Try.

Stay.

I should say no. Mama is waiting with dinner. I have a speech to polish for the next district outreach, our biggest with a dozen *barangay* involved.

But the car door is already open. The night smells like rain waiting for permission to fall.

"Fifteen minutes," I say.

He smiles like I said forever.

We drive aimlessly through the early evening traffic.

Windows down. Air thick with the coming storm.

"Why do you fight so much?" I ask.

"Because it feels like proof," he says. "Like if I hit hard enough, the world will hit back and at least then I'll know it sees me."

"That's the stupidest thing I've ever heard."

"Yeah?" He glances at me. "Why do you work so much?"

"Because it feels like protection," I say before I can edit it. "If I have a plan, then at least the world has to argue with me in bullet points. I'm prepared for it."

He laughs. "Wow. Look at us. Two completely different coping mechanisms. One disaster."

"Speak for yourself."

"Princess," he says, almost fondly. "You are the most beautiful disaster I've ever seen."

I look out at the city streets. *Sari-sari* stores lit like tiny altars, people ducking into tricycles with plastic bags looped over hair, a kid in a Superman shirt hopping over potholes like lava.

"Pull over," I say.

He does, under a flickering streetlamp that buzzes like an insect with secrets.

We sit in the loud quiet of a car cooling down. His breath is rough. Mine is worse.

"Don't," I say.

"I didn't do anything."

"You're about to."

He chuckles, then sobers almost immediately. "I'm really not good for you."

"Tell me something I don't know."

"And you're the best thing that's happened to me in a long time."

"I know that, too," I say, and the honesty hurts more than the bruise on his face.

We look at each other until the light from the streetlamp steadies and the shadows fall.

Then he kisses me.

It's always the same first second. It's like falling into a well I watched him dig.

The second after that is different every time. This one tastes like the coming storm. This one tastes like apologies we will not say. This one tastes like the mouth you only have when you think you're about to be forgiven for what you could never be.

His hand cups my jaw. My fingers knot in the collar of his shirt. He pulls me closer, a little too hard. I let him. I kiss him back, a little harder.

When we pull apart, my breath shivers.

"You can't keep doing this," I tell him, still panting a little.

"Doing what?"

"Picking fights. Getting hurt. Dragging me into your mess."

He huffs a laugh that isn't funny. "Dragging you in? You dive, babe."

"Don't call me 'babe.'"

"What should I call you then?"

"Nothing," I say, voice sharp. "Or my name. Or President, if you want to be annoying. Annoying I can deal with."

"President it is." He leans in again, close enough that I can see the pulse leap at his throat. "You're shaking."

"Because you make me so mad."

"That's not why."

"Maybe it is."

"Maybe," he says, because he knows when not to push. He pulls back, puts the car in gear, drives me home.

At my curb he doesn't say goodnight. I don't say stay. We never do.

When I get to my room, I press my palm to the middle of my chest.

I count.

Beat. Beat.

Then silence.

That pause fills with his name, with the shape of his smile, with the stupid tilt of his head. I tell myself it's just adrenaline.

I tell myself it's not love. I tell myself the bruise blooming on my mouth is blotted lipstick.

I tell myself to sleep.

I tell myself to stop.

Our outreach drive hums like a machine I built from stubbornness. People line up. Kids grab bread with both hands and run away laughing. The seniors get their blood pressure taken and tell me stories I didn't ask for but need.

He is there, hauling boxes like they're lighter in his hands than they really are. Sweat slicks the hair at his neck. Volunteers orbit him—half wary, half drawn.

I hate that watching him makes my teeth ache.

When it starts to drizzle, he looks up at the sky like an old friend and grins.

I feel it tug painfully at the inside of my stomach.

"Great job, President," he says later, hoisting the last crate into the van.

"Thank you," I say to the van, because if I look at him he'll know what I really mean.

He waits. He's patient in the exact ways that hurt me.

"You coming to the concert after?" he asks. "Your beloved cultural hour?"

"It's not an hour," I say. "But yes. A lot of alumni will be there."

"Save me a seat?"

"You never sit," I say, smiling without meaning to. "You lurk."

"Then save me a place to lurk."

"I don't reserve corners."

"For me you always do," he says. "Even if you won't admit it."

It's too close to the truth, and I hate him for it.

Instead of raising funds, the cultural concert raises chaos like Murphy's Law.

Lights misbehave. A microphone squeaks and refuses to work since. One of the performers is running late from a traffic accident across town.

My vice president whispers that the head of the alumni association is here, which means we have to look like we know what we're doing if we want the funds to expand the College of Management library.

He appears in the wings like a problem I forgot to solve.

He lurks, as always.

"You look like a headline," he says, taking in my suit, my too-sleek hair, my pale face and my trembling hands. "All caps."

"And you look like a bad idea," I say. "In italics. Ripped jeans? Really?"

He laughs. "You're funny when you're stressed."

"I'm funny when you're around," I snap. "It's a symptom."

"Of what?"

"Poor judgment."

"On a scale of one to disaster," he murmurs, leaning in, "how bad is it tonight?"

I nearly tell him it's catastrophic, but I really want to say: *Old habit, new bruise.*

Instead I say, "Get back to your corner. Keep lurking. You're good at it."

He salutes, backs away, but his eyes snag on the soloist walking past, Alton from the debate club, a perfectly decent boy who sometimes carries my laptop after team meetings.

Alton nods at me, friendly. "Good luck, Bea. Break a leg. Or whatever presidents do."

I smile. "Thanks."

"Who's that?" he asks after Alton passes, voice suddenly flat.

"Don't start."

"I asked you a question."

"You're not my boyfriend."

"That's convenient," he says, mouth tight.

"For both of us," I say. "Focus, please. There are donors and alumni present. Try not to fight anyone tonight. *Please.*"

He snorts, but his eyes are still on Alton. I feel the heat of something ugly unfurl from him.

The performances start with a traditional *rondalla*. The lights go up. The city outside exhales rain against the roof.

We almost make it through the first half of the show.

Between acts, Alton jokes with a technician about the old, wobbly microphone stand and casually claps my shoulder as he passes. I feel the weight of his stare like a hand around my throat.

"Hey," he says, stepping in front of Alton. "Watch your hands."

Alton blinks at him in confusion. "What?"

"I saw you," he says. "Hands. Shoulder. Watch it."

"Are you serious, bro?" Alton laughs, looking to me for help.

"Backstage isn't the place," I say, stepping between them. "Please. Both of you."

Alton lifts both palms and backs away, irritation written clean across his face.

He steps closer. "You let him touch you?"

"He didn't touch me," I hiss. "He's my teammate. This is my event. You don't get to be a scene in it."

Something flickers in his eyes.

Hurt, maybe. Fast as lightning, then gone just as quickly.

"You never pick me," he says quietly.

It's the truest thing he's ever said.

"I pick what needs me," I retort.

And it's the truest thing I've ever said.

He flinches like I swung a bat and it smacked him right across the face.

He doesn't say or do anything for a few long seconds. Then he takes a deep breath.

"I'm going." The words leave his mouth like the rain outside the auditorium.

He disappears before I can decide whether to follow or not.

I run the rest of the show on autopilot. My brain is a list, but my chest is a wound.

When it's over, when the alumni shake my hand and say words like *promise* and *potential* and *allocations,* I smile like the kind of girl who never chooses wrong. I go to the parking lot and breathe dark air that smells like wet asphalt and exhaustion.

He is there, of course, smoking a cigarette, sitting on the hood of his car that still bears traces of the downpour.

"Congrats, President," he mutters.

"I told you not to start something. You promised me one night without drama."

"I didn't promise anything," he says. "I don't know how."

"You made me a liar," I say. "You made me choose between my job and you and you're mad I didn't pick you in the middle of a live show."

He laughs humorlessly, then rubs a hand over his face, cigarette between fingers. "I didn't make you do anything. You never let me make you do anything."

"So what is this?" I demand, pain blooming into anger. "What do you want from me? A schedule? A curfew? A leash?"

He takes a step closer.

Then grabs my wrist.

It's not hard. It's not gentle either.

But it's enough to leave the ghost of his fingers on my skin tomorrow morning.

"Don't ever talk about leashes to me," he says, voice

dangerously low "You have no idea what it's like to be…to be—"

"Owned?" I say, because I know about his father and the belt and the way he learned to take pain without moving. "I know. That's why I'm still here."

"Then be here," he begs. "Like now. Pick me now. Bea, please."

"I can't pick you when you're like this, Mike! How could I?"

"When I'm like what?

"When you're hurting yourself by trying to hurt someone else first."

He lets go like my skin burned him. He turns and punches the concrete wall. The sound is like a crack of thunder. He bites back a swear word and a groan.

"Great," I say numbly. "Now you're bleeding."

"Don't," he says. "Don't pity me. Don't fix me. Just don't."

"Then what do you want?"

He looks at me then. His face is stone, but his eyes are filled with the fire of terror.

"I want you to love me when I'm not easy. Because that's the only version of me I know how to be."

I take a step back, inwardly flailing.

Then I hear it.

My heart thundering right back.

A beat. A pulse. Another.

The space between them fills with all the things I could say and don't.

"I do," I whisper. "That's the problem."

We stand inside the fallout of that confession.

"Come with me," he says suddenly. "Just for tonight. We'll drive nowhere. We'll get the best *inasal* for dinner with what's left of my money. We can be bad at this together and maybe that makes it good."

"I have to lock up," I say. "I have to sign forms for the equipment. I have to—"

"You always 'have to,'" he says, the words breaking. "You always put me after the list."

"And you always ask me to be the kind of girl who doesn't keep promises."

He laughs once, the sound bitter and ugly. "So we're done."

"I didn't say that."

"You didn't have to."

He gets in his car and leaves rubber and the threat of tears on the wet pavement.

I press my hand to my chest and count.

Beat. Beat.

Then silence.

But I can hear it howl.

For two days, he doesn't text.

I sleep badly and do my job too well and pretend I don't look up every time a gray car rumbles past the university gate.

I walk through my classes like a zombie on crack. I even ace a surprise exam.

But I still hear the howling in my emptiness.

On the third night, he calls just before the clock strikes twelve.

"Hey," he says, voice hoarse. "I'm at the court. The one near the river."

"It's midnight," I answer automatically, a little breathless.

"I know."

"What do you need?"

He chuckles softly. "You."

I sit down on the floor next to my bed before my knees give out. "Is your father—"

"Not tonight. Just…come?"

I go. I don't tell anyone. I throw a jacket over my plain shirt and cotton pants, and tie my hair and run.

The ride-share man doesn't ask any questions. He only plays Bee Gees songs on his stereo as he drives, careful not to catch my eye.

He's sitting cross-legged at center court, hood up, shoulders hunched. The court lights paint him in faint silver.

I sit beside him without a word.

"You always come," he says, not looking at me.

"That's not true."

"Don't lie to me on my favorite court. Especially not tonight."

I rest my head on his shoulder. He lets me. His breath shakes a little.

"I'm sorry," he whispers into the dark. "About the show. About Alton. About everything."

"Stop apologizing for everything," I say. "Pick one thing and be specific."

He huffs out a small laugh. "I'm sorry I grabbed your wrist."

"Thank you," I say. "I'm sorry I made you feel like my job matters more than you."

"It should," he says. "It's the version of you that makes sense. It's what makes you…you, I guess."

"I want the version that loves you to make sense too."

He turns his face into my hair, gently pulling off the rubber band from my ponytail. "Me too."

We sit there, bodies leaning like battered trees in the same storm. The river hums to itself behind the court. A dog barks twice, then decides to give us peace and quiet.

"Do you think we can do this?" he asks. "Like people do? Not like a movie, or a disaster? Just…dates and fights that don't end in bleeding and broken things. And maybe one day I show up to a concert and clap like a normal person. I may decide not to lurk anymore. What do you think?"

"I don't know," I answer honestly. "But I want to try."

"Okay," he says. "Then let's try."

For one fragile moment, it feel as if we built a bridge out of the worst of us.

It feels as if the world might just let us cross.

For once.

Trying lasts exactly eight days.

For eight days he texts before he shows up. He stops smoking, then starts again, then stops. He puts ice on his knuckles instead of punching anything. He comes to dinner at our house and tells my mother about the houses he wants to build for people who don't get houses. My mother smiles at him with soft eyes I have never seen her use on a boy.

On the ninth day he is late to my intercollegiate debate final and I am okay. On the tenth he is even later to my presentation to the alumni association—and I am not.

On the eleventh day he does not come at all.

He calls at midnight.

He is crying and drunk and at the court again, and the old anger and the old tenderness tear my ribcage in half.

"I needed you there," I say, voice flat and tight with trying not to sob. "For once, I needed you."

"I'm sorry," he says. "I got into it with—" He stops. "I messed up. Again. I don't know why I keep choosing wrong."

"You do," I say, and the cruelty surprises me. "Because it's the only way you know you're still…you."

Silence. The kind that lands with heavy finality.

Then he says, in a small, almost childlike voice, "Don't leave."

"I'm not," I answer quietly. "I'm finally staying with myself."

He makes a noise like a boy broken in half. "Please, Bea. Please."

"I love you," I say. It sounds like it's both mercy and pain.

"I love you so much it's destroying me," I continue. "At times…I even want it to."

"Then let it," he says, with sudden fierceness. "Let it destroy you. Let it destroy both of us."

"I can't, Mike. I can't."

There it is.

The choice that has been waiting like a wolf at the edge of the dark forest.

I listen to him breathe. Maybe for the last time.

"Okay," he says after what seems like forever. "Okay."

We hang up.

I press my hand to my chest and count.

Beat. Beat.

Silence.

In it, I feel something close. Not the love. Not the want. The door that lets me live.

We meet one last time, because endings deserve daylight.

At the footbridge over the *estero* near the university, the early morning sun glinting off water that pretends to be clean, he leans against the rail wearing the same dark hoodie from the court, hair a mess, eyes milked out from not sleeping.

"You look like hell," I say, because love has always been cruelty wrapped in care.

"You look like the truth," he says, because he always returns it with something I don't know where to put.

People move around us, caught in their own little worlds.

A woman in scrubs, a man holding a cake like it's a baby, a teenager in a school uniform practicing a speech under his breath.

"We're not good," I tell him honestly.

"We could be," he says.

I hear the hope he knows better than to feed.

But it's too late for that kind of thing now.

"I don't mean ever," I say. "I mean right now. This version."

He nods, hands jammed into the pockets of his ripped jeans. "I know."

"Say the thing," I ask softly. "The honest version."

He sighs. "I don't know how to love you without making you smaller than the thing I'm trying to survive."

I swallow hard at that.

"And I don't know how to love you," I answer, "without trying to turn you into the kind of person I can take to a donor dinner."

He laughs, but the sound shatters softly midway. "God. We're really bad at this."

"Not always," I say, smiling because it's true. "Sometimes we were perfect."

He nods. "The car. The court. Even the rain."

"The dinner," I add. "The almost."

"The almost," he echoes.

We stand there, two people who did not manage to keep the bridge from collapsing.

But we know—there really was a bridge. Even if it wasn't meant to last.

"Can I ask one more thing?" he says.

I nod. "Just one."

Because I know boundaries are pieces of love dressed in armor.

"Kiss me," he says.

The way he says it is not a demand. It's a prayer.

I step close. I cup his face, careful of old bruises and fresh cracks, gentle to the point of cruelty. I kiss him slowly, almost dreamily—mouth soft, breath slow, the shape of us simple for once.

It's the kind of kiss you give to broken things.

His hands stay at his sides, but I feel him tremble.

When I pull back we both laugh, not because it's funny but because surviving it is.

"Thank you," he says.

"Don't thank me," I say. "Just…take care."

He nods.

He will try.

I will try.

We will both fail and then try again for people who are not each other.

I nod back, feeling the tears sloshing behind my lids.

I walk away first. I don't look back.

At the far end of the bridge, I press two fingers to my wrist and count.

Beat. Beat.

Then silence.

In that pause, he lives.

Not as a wound. Not as a man I'm waiting on. But as a color under the skin, fading and permanent at once. As proof that I loved like the worst and best parts of me learned at the same time.

A bruise-colored love.

I still remember him that way.

In the silence between heartbeats, he stays.

Where the ache is honest, where the lesson is clean, where I am whole enough to choose the next person with both hands.

Where I know I will not be destroyed from that love.

But I never forget.

CHAPTER 3

The Ones We Don't Choose

The girl who knows too much.

That's what they called me in school. Not in the affectionate way, either. The smart girl. The overachiever. The one with the sharp answers, the clean handwriting, the perfectly bulleted list of expectations.

I was the girl who solved equations before anyone else finished reading the problem. The one who joined debates for fun, the one who fixed group projects alone because no one else could meet the standard I set.

And he was the boy who didn't say much.

Not stupid, though. Never stupid.

Just…quiet. The kind of quiet that wasn't detachment, but study. Thought. Stillness. He had eyes like dusk. They were brown, then gray; soft, unassuming, but impossible to ignore once you realized they were watching everything.

He always sat at the back. Always hunched, as if trying to hide how tall he really was. Always with a pen poised over his notebook, but never raising his hand.

And I fell for him anyway. Or maybe because of it.

"You should talk more," I told him once.

We were sitting in the library. Our school library wasn't big, just three rows of shelves and a corner table with a chipped leg, but it was always empty after exams.

Everyone else was at the canteen. We were there, solving practice sheets for fun, trying to remember the questions and to figure out if we got the answers right.

My kind of fun.

He looked up from his notes. "Why?"

"Because people might think you're arrogant."

He gave the smallest shrug. "Let them."

I nudged the open page in front of him. He'd solved the most complicated fraction problem in three steps.

"You're not," I said.

He looked at me for a long time. Not in the way boys usually did—not sizing me up, not undressing me with his eyes, not comparing me to someone else. He looked like he was storing the moment in his head, his eyes of dusk taking a snapshot of what we were and never will be again.

"You're the only one who knows me," he said.

"Oh?"

"You know me in a way other people don't. I don't know why, but you do."

Then I felt it. Somewhere beneath my ribs. That quiet blooming.

The first time he kissed me was in the hallway outside the science lab.

We were sixteen. Everyone else had gone home. I was ranting about the interschool sports rankings being weighted unfairly. He was nodding like he always did, letting me spin out, letting me burn.

I turned to him, in the middle of a sentence, and he kissed me.

No warning. No buildup. Just his hand curling around my wrist and his mouth on mine, warm and a little wet.

When he pulled back, I was breathless.

"Slow down," he said quietly.

And I did.

But my heart was racing like an engine without brakes.

The summer we finished school, I heard he got accepted to the Criminology program of a university in the city.

No warning. No buildup.

Just a text that said, *Might become a cop, after all.*

I called him. He didn't pick up.

I saw him three days later, standing at the bus terminal with a duffel bag and a buzz cut. He looked like someone who had already left.

"Why?" I asked, swallowing the rest of the words.

All the plans, all the promises. All the *almosts* and *what-ifs.*

He looked away. "It seemed…simple."

"Nothing about you is simple, Chris."

He met my eyes then. Really met them.

I hated how calm he looked. He looked like he'd rehearsed this moment in his head until it no longer hurt.

I hate how his eyes still look like the dusk I always loved.

"That's the problem," he said.

I only stared back.

The conductor hopped onto the bus step, and called out the city.

"Goodbye, Pearl," he said, hesitating before kissing my cheek.

He pressed a notebook into my hand.

And then he was gone.

I stood watching the yellow vehicle until it disappeared into the winding mountain roads.

At first, he wrote emails.

Sparse like him. Sentences with no embellishment. No pictures.

Just thoughts.

I'm still here.

It's loud in the dorm. But it's silent inside.

Saw a dog today that looked like the one we fed fries behind the gym. Made me laugh.

Dreamt of the library. You were scolding me for chewing my protractor.

I heard your favorite song on the radio. I sang it for the boys at videoke. Don't know why.

I wrote back in perfectly typed paragraphs.

I told him everything. My schedule, my theories, what books I was reading. I painstakingly took photos, in all the right light and angles. I attached memes I thought he'd find funny.

I poured myself into each message, hoping he'd feel me there.

He never said *I miss you*. Not once.

But he ended one email with this: *The quiet here is heavy. I miss your noise.*

I read that line until it blurred on the screen. Or maybe until I got all teary-eyed from staring.

The emails stopped after his second year.

I don't know why.

Maybe the silence stopped missing me.

It's five years before I see him again.

I'm buying vegetables for my mother at the public market. It's hot. The air is thick with smoke and chatter.

And suddenly, there he is.

Still tall. Broader now, with a sharper jaw and shorter hair.

His eyes remain familiar.

Dusk. And stillness.

A girl walks beside him.

She's wearing a simple pink sundress with green leaves at the hem. Shoulder-length hair pulled back with a clip. She has soft, slender arms and a sweet smile.

The kind of girl who probably doesn't argue about technicalities. The kind who probably doesn't have a five-year plan or a ten-year vision board.

He sees me.

"Hey, Pearl," he says, the words stumbling into each other.

He looks startled, like he'd just run into a memory he wasn't expecting to remember.

"Hey," I say. "How are you, Chris?"

The girl smiles at me politely, regarding me with curious eyes.

He doesn't introduce us.

We talk in fragments.

"You're back."

"Yeah. Settled in the next town. I work for the station there. You can say I'm very lucky to get a chance like that. See the family often."

The girl glances between us, then nods.

"You look well," I tell him.

"So do you."

His hand settles on the girl's back. Familiar, almost automatic.

"Are you still…in school?" he asks.

"Grad school," I say. "Public Administration. The

Congressman gave me a scholarship. I'm his Information Officer. I visit Mama on the weekends when I don't have work or exams."

He nods. Of course. That tracks. I am still too much.

The girl walks ahead to look at a fish stall.

I turn to him. "Why her?"

He doesn't flinch or even look surprised.

He just looks…tired. Worn, even.

"She's…easy."

I laugh bitterly. "And I wasn't?"

He shakes his head. "You were everything. Too much of everything. I didn't know how to carry it all without breaking."

"So you chose less."

"I chose what I could keep."

The words come down like a landslide, but I'm still breathing.

I nod, trying to find the in-between of peace and letting go. "She seems nice."

"She is. We'll be having our first baby, hopefully in five months."

"Congratulations," I say automatically.

"Thanks," he answers, just as quickly.

I swallow past the lump in my throat. "I hope you're happy, Chris. I really do."

He clears his own. I think at first he's not going to say anything more.

"You made me feel seen," he says at last, voice so low I almost miss it. "But she makes me feel safe."

I don't respond. There's nothing left to say.

The girl returns with a bag of *tilapia* and takes his hand.

"Great bargain," I say to her.

"Isn't it?" she answers with a grin. "I can make this last three days."

He looks at me one last time as they walk away.

That night, I sit on my bedroom floor with his old notebook. The one he left behind when he left town.

The pages are full of half-solved problems and my notes in the margins, bossy and bright.

I run my hand over the paper.

My heart beats quickly for two counts, then falls silent.

And in that silence, I think of him.

Not the man who chose safety.

Not the husband. Not the cop.

The boy who let me talk without interrupting.

The one who kissed me mid-sentence.

The one who said, *"You're the only one who knows me."*

The one who wrote he dreamt of me in the library.

That version of him only lived in a narrow space, a window in time between ambition and simplicity, between noise and surrender, between love and choice.

And I still live there, sometimes.

In the space between then and now, between the first heartbeat and the one that follows.

Remembering the ones we don't choose.

Or the ones who didn't choose us.

CHAPTER 4

The Light in the Window

I DON'T KNOW WHO HE IS.

I don't even know what he does for a living.

Not for the first three months, anyway.

But I know that he makes coffee at exactly 6:04 every morning. I know that he reads by the window with his feet curled under him like a cat. I know that he waters his plants every three days, even if it rains. I know that he leaves his window open during thunderstorms, but unrolls a makeshift tarp to keep the wind and water out.

And I know that his lamp glows until almost midnight, flicking off a few seconds before mine.

I don't mean to watch. Not at first. I only notice because his apartment is across from mine—diagonal, close enough to see into when the curtains are open, far enough that the details blur.

He's quiet, almost gentle, by nature. He doesn't play loud music or have people over. He moves like he doesn't want to bother the floor.

In a city that's crowded, loud, and constantly moving, his quiet is magnetic.

I call him Window Boy in my head.

Window Boy with his thick black hair almost always tousled, with his slightly lopsided silver-rimmed glasses.

I know how he looks the same way I know my favorite digital print.

The first time we acknowledge each other, it's barely more than a glance. Or maybe a blink exchange.

I'm standing by my kitchen counter with a bowl of noodles. It's almost midnight. I look up, and he's at his window, watching the rain.

He sees me.

I see him.

We freeze at the same time.

A heartbeat of stillness.

Then, shyly, he lifts his hand. He gives me a small, tentative wave.

I wave back.

He smiles. Just a little.

Just enough.

That night, I sleep better than I have in weeks.

We fall into a rhythm.

We wave in the mornings now. I sip my awful green tea, he sips coffee.

Sometimes I hold up a book, and he nods like he approves.

Once, he held up a notebook with a post-it stuck to it that said, *"What are you reading today?"*

I wrote my answer on printer paper and held it up. *"Never Let Me Go, Kazuo Ishiguro."*

He made a little heart with his hands.

I decide he's a little bit of a nerd, just like me.

It was stupid. And sweet.

It made my whole day quieter in the best way.

If this is peace, then I want it.

I learn his habits. He likes chicken-flavored instant noodles with egg. He folds laundry with perfect corners, always starting with the largest pieces. He takes his time drinking his coffee, inhaling and sipping in turn, causing his glasses to fog up.

He learns mine too. He knows when I'm working late. He knows when I'm too tired to cook and eat crackers at the window instead. He knows when I'm sad, even if I'm smiling.

I can tell because he sends a small, thoughtful gesture across the distance. Sometimes it's a thumbs up or a peace sign; other times it's a paper swan or a slightly wilted flower stuck to the glass.

I keep a journal now, a weird little A4 document online that I update every day before bed. The template is a rich pink, bordered with white hearts and fluffy cats.

Day 42: He wore blue again. The good blue. The soft one.

Day 55: We both held up ramen at the same time. It felt like a conversation.

Day 61: He waved goodnight. I waved back late. He waited. He didn't even move from his spot.

I don't write about work. Or my family. Or my loneliness. I only write about him.

One night, the storm hits hard.

The kind that knocks power out in entire blocks with one strong gust.

My apartment goes dark. I scramble for candles. For a moment, the city feels swallowed.

I move to the window out of habit.

His apartment is dark too.

But then, a flashlight flicks on.

He's there, holding it up. It casts a soft beam in the shape of a smile.

I lift my candle.

He sits by the window with it, just holding the light between us.

We stay like that for almost an hour, two shadows in the dark, watching the storm unravel.

I press my hand to the glass.

After a moment, he does the same.

Our palms don't touch, not really. But I feel something pass through the pane.

A stillness. A warmth.

A maybe.

The first note appears two days later.

In plain white paper, folded and taped to my door. The handwriting inside is neat, slender, and no-nonsense.

"Hi. I'm Winston. I'm sorry if it's weird, but I asked the security guard which unit had the girl who always reads in the window. I'd like to know your name. If that's okay."

"PS: You have excellent taste in instant noodles."

I laugh so loudly I scare my neighbor's cat. It gives me a judgmental stare before padding off down the corridor.

I write back.

"Hi Winston. I'm Charlene. And yes, it's okay. I've been calling you Window Boy in my head, so this is a huge upgrade."

"PPS: I have excellent taste in many things."

The next day, a new note appears.

"I'm sure you do. Want to prove it? Coffee?"

Our first real, face-to-face conversation doesn't happen until three weeks later.

We meet at the corner café a block away.

He's taller in person. Warm and good-natured, but nervous in a way that makes me feel braver.

His good blue shirt is slightly untucked from his jeans in one corner.

I decide, right then and there, that I like him.

We talk for three hours. About everything. About nothing. It's easy.

He listens like I'm a song he's trying to learn by heart.

When we say goodbye, he doesn't kiss me.

He just gives my hand a quick squeeze and says, "I'll see you at the window."

And I do.

Every day. Every night.

It's like clockwork. A comfort I almost crave like air, something I didn't know I needed until it was right there through the glass.

We fall in love through the window.

With scribbled signs. With matching cups. With watching the same movie and reacting in real time, holding up rating cards we made for each other. Mine has his choice of old laptop cardboard boxes cut into squares; his are colored pink and decorated with fluffy cats in varying moods.

We meet on weekends. We get takeout and hang out at his place.

We take long walks in the neighborhood. Somehow, it always happens right after there's rain, when it feels like something's coming back to life.

In late-night conversations, he tells me things slowly, almost thoughtfully. I learn not to rush the quiet.

He kisses me in the elevator once, just before the doors open for him to step out. I giggle for three floors afterward. My neighbor's cat judges me once more, but I can see the grudging approval now.

One time, after sharing a bucket of fried chicken for dinner, he brushes a strand of hair behind my ear like it's the most natural thing in the world.

It is.

The day we say *I love you*, it happens at the window.

No theatrics. No music.

Just two people holding up signs at the same time, accidentally, ridiculously in sync.

On white cardboard, his says: *"I think I'm falling for you."*

On a pink A4 with fluffy cats, mine answers: *"I already love you."*

We both start laughing. Then crying. Then laughing again.

Later, he comes over and kisses me like my laughter is a secret he finally knows.

And I think maybe we always knew this was going to happen.

From the very first wave. From the first silence we filled together.

Now, I watch him sleep on my couch. He fell asleep halfway through a movie. His coffee's gone cold on the table. His glasses slide down his nose.

I take a blanket from the closet and tuck it around his long limbs. I take his glasses off and put it carefully on the table.

I kiss him on the lips, then rise slowly.

Even though he's here with me, I press my hand to the window.

Out of habit. Out of gratitude.

I can see it's drizzling.

The apartment across from mine is dark now. It looks still, but not empty. Not really.

It's filled with the silence between two heartbeats.

It's full of memory. Of promise. Of waiting.

Of my love for my Window Boy.

And this time, when I reach for the glass, I feel him put his palm over my knuckles.

His other arm goes around my waist. He presses his lips to my hair.

"Hi," he murmurs.

"Hi," I echo.

He feels warm.

Real. Close enough to hold.

At last.

CHAPTER 5

Sun and Steel

They say I'm too loud, too smart, too soft, too fat, too bright.

You can say I'm too much of everything.

And yet he barely speaks at all.

When I first meet him, he's the new gym instructor at the local wellness center where I work part-time.

He walks like he used to belong to something stricter, something stronger. He stands like he's waiting for orders that don't come anymore.

His arms are built like stone. He's always in black.

There's a scar across his left eyebrow. And a silence around him so thick it feels like history.

"You're not what I expected," I tell him after our third hallway pass.

He blinks. "What did you expect?"

"More…gym. Less assassin."

"Arys." He follows the name with the ghost of a smile. "Almost Marine."

That catches me. His face softens; his eyes crinkle at the corners, almost kindly.

I don't realize I stopped breathing for a second.

"Laurie," I answer, feeling a flush rise up my throat. "Almost lawyer."

He tells me later, when we're alone by the back stairwell during break time, that he didn't make it. He trained, enlisted, prepped. But then the migraines started. Then the blackouts. Then the diagnosis: a benign but inoperable growth near his brain stem. Not deadly. Not curable. Just…a permanent no.

"The body was willing," he says. "But the brain had other plans."

He says it like a joke. I hear the heartbreak in it.

I tell him about law school being put on indefinite pause.

"My dad passed away," I say. "A tumor in his throat. A year later, my mom followed. It was her breast this time. Life had other plans."

He nods solemnly. "I'm sorry."

I nod in thanks.

And when I do, he reaches for a lock of my hair, rolling it over his fingers.

Then he lets go.

I swallow hard and walk back into the center.

But his touch stays with me.

We become a strange kind of constant.

I start showing up early. I bring him coffee and fresh *puto* from the market.

We stay late, talking. I watch him train like he's still trying to earn a title he lost.

I start walking and stretching more. I ask him to show me routines.

It's not about weight at first. It's about strength. About being in my body and not apologizing for it.

But then he says, quietly, during a plank hold, "You're glowing lately."

Something inside me stirs. Just a little, but I feel it.

I start pushing harder.

He never asks me to. Never hints that he wants me to shrink. But I see how his eyes change when I walk into a room. How they linger longer.

And I want him to want me.

Not just as I am, but because I can be more.

More of the world he understands. Less of the softness that makes people underestimate me.

So I keep pushing.

We kiss for the first time after a staff party, when he drops me off at my boardinghouse.

I'm in a dress I never would have worn six months ago. It's form-hugging, nipped at the waist and bare at the arms. The dipped neckline teases what I've always been secretly proud of.

He looks at me like he's never seen me before.

"You clean up nice," he says.

"I was always nice."

"You were always beautiful," he replies.

I don't know what to do with that truth, so I lean in. My hand lands in the middle of his chest.

He leans down, all shadow and warmth.

The kiss is slow. It feels gentle. Honest.

It feels like a pact to break through each other's walls.

We make love one week later.

It happens in his tiny apartment. On his neatly-made bed.

The heat comes from his silence, his steely focus on what he could make me feel.

I tremble when I take my shirt off.

Not because I'm scared, but because this matters. Because this is the body I live in. The body I've fought with and fed and punished and tried to make smaller.

The body he touches like it is a gift.

He doesn't say anything when I cry. He just kisses my shoulders, and holds me so gently I almost fall apart.

And when we move together, it's feels as if we're made for this rhythm.

We sleep tangled, limbs soft and sore, our breath syncing in the dark.

I think it's the beginning of something.

It isn't.

He starts pulling away two months later.

Not cruelly. Just…less.

Shorter replies. Longer silences. Distance growing cobwebs in all the places we used to be close.

When I ask him if something's wrong, he shakes his head.

"Nothing's wrong. You're amazing. I'm just…tired."

I want to scream.

I want to ask if it's me. If I lost too much. If I lost what made me his.

If I'll never be enough, even if I lost it all.

But I don't.

But I think I already know.

I see it in the way he looks at the ocean when we pass it in his battered blue car. He looks like he's still out there, in a version of himself that didn't break. A version of him that wasn't told he couldn't be someone.

In a life where I was only a passing glance, a girl full and loud—not the girl who stayed.

We end things in the center's parking lot.

He doesn't cry. Neither do I.

He says, "You changed me."

I say, "You made me want to change."

He holds my face for a long time. "You'll find someone, Laurie. Someone better."

I laugh, because it's the last thing that's funny. "No one will be better. Just different."

He kisses my lips, then my forehead.

I reach up to caress the scar on his eyebrow.

"Goodbye, Arys."

And then he's gone.

A week later, he quits his job.

After a year, I meet someone else.

A science teacher at a private all-boys school, with messy hair and gentle hands who listens when I talk about starting law school again. He answers perfectly, and shares with me his plans to take his Doctorate in Education.

We start slow.

He likes to hold my hand. I let him.

When we kiss, I don't compare it.

But sometimes, in the quiet, I remember.

The push of muscle against mine.

The silence of a man who wanted to be steel and unbreakable and couldn't forgive himself for failing.

The first time I say *I love you* to the man I'm with now, he says it back without pause.

A week later, his sister, a friend who works out at the gym, tells me he's been looking at rings on layaway.

And still, I go to my room and cry in the shower.

Because love can be good and still not be first.

Because Arys taught me how to glow.

Because I still remember him.

The soldier who never was.

The man who kissed me like I was made of the sun.

The steely silence where I learned I could love without disappearing.

Even if it isn't him.

CHAPTER 6

A Second-Chance Life

THEY TELL ME I SHOULD FEEL GRATEFUL.

A second chance. A new life. A heart that beats strong and steady inside my chest when my old one stuttered, failed, and gave up.

Sometimes, gratitude tastes like guilt. Sometimes, I can't sleep without imagining the girl who died so I could live.

I don't know her name. The donor registry doesn't allow that.

But I know I feel her. In the way my breath catches at songs I've never heard before. In the dreams that are not mine. In the strange ache I get when I walk past the pier for the first time after the surgery.

I thought I was going crazy. Until I met him.

His name is Jay.

He's a barista at this music-themed indie coffee shop I wandered into one afternoon after a panic attack in the hospital parking lot. The kind of place with paintings by local artists on the walls and a small raised platform in the front for open mic nights.

I was hiding in a corner, hands shaking around my cup, when he slid me a small piece of banana bread without a word.

I didn't even look at him until I tasted it.

It was the best banana bread I'd ever had.

And I started crying.

"Hey," he said softly. "It's not that bad."

He had kind eyes. Almost sad.

"I'm sorry," I mumbled, brushing tears off my face. "I just…this tastes like home. And I don't know why. Seriously, though, I've lived in this city my whole life. So…it feels weird."

He didn't laugh. Just tilted his head and said, "Maybe it's reminding you of someone."

And maybe, just maybe, something in me remembered him.

I keep coming back.

Every Tuesday and Thursday, between physical therapy and checkups, I sit in the same corner, drink the same iced coffee, eat the same banana bread he doesn't charge me for.

We start talking.

He's gentle, sometimes funny. He orbits my corner almost protectively, like a bouncer for bad vibes.

He's the kind of boy who never pushes when I'm not ready to talk, but always makes space for whatever I have to share.

I finally tell him I'd had a transplant.

He just nods, like I made perfect sense.

Then one day, he tells me, "My sister loved banana bread. I used to bake it for her every Sunday. I guess the owner here liked it too."

My throat closes.

I don't know why I ask, "What happened to her?"

Because I think…I already know.

He smiles, a small one. His eyes look broken and haunted.

"Car accident," he answers. "Jana signed up to be a donor when she turned eighteen. Said if anything ever happened, she wanted to help someone else live. Lost her last July. I've been on my own since. She kind of raised me."

July.

My hand goes to my chest.

And now, I think he knows too.

"I think I've been looking for you," I say softly.

Jay doesn't cry, but his eyes shimmer in the dim light.

"You feel it too?" he asks. "Sometimes I dream of her. And she's…smiling, but always walking away. I thought I was going crazy. But when I met you, I swear I saw her again."

I nod. "She's still here. Somewhere. And maybe she brought me to you."

He reaches across the table and takes my hand in his.

His touch feels warm and soft, like the foam on top of my favorite iced cappuccino.

"I think Jana would be happy," he said. "Knowing her heart found you."

And that's when the weight in my chest lifts.

For the first time since the surgery, I seem to find my heartbeat again.

We don't fall in love all at once.

It's not cinematic. There are no grand declarations.

Just stolen glances. Just slow, healing conversations.

We share books and music. We take late-night walks at the port, where Jana used to busk during tourist season.

Above all, the simple joy of finding home in someone else's heartbeat.

I tell my doctors I feel stronger. I tell Jay I finally feel real.

I finally feel alive.

Sometimes, he plays his sister's favorite songs on the coffee shop speakers. I dance while helping him mop the floors after closing.

Sometimes, when it's cooler, we sit at the pier and he tells me stories about her.

Sometimes, we don't say anything at all. Just hold each other, feeling the steady rhythm that once belonged to someone else.

It's been a year.

I leave the hospital for the last time. No more checkups. No more monitors. Just me, alive and scarred and smiling.

Jay's waiting by the doors with a bouquet of daisies and stargazer lilies in his hand. The same daisies his sister used to draw on his notebooks.

But the lilies…they're all me.

"You ready?" he asks.

I tilt my head, the smile not leaving my face. "For what?"

He grins. "Everything."

I take his hand—and I say the words.

"I love you."

His arms wrap around me, squishing the bouquet a little bit, but I don't mind.

"I love you, too, Cindy."

And my heart—her heart—beats strong.

For the first time, it feels like it's mine.

And I know, wherever she is, she's not gone.

She lives in us.

In our love.

A love we found in banana bread and healing.

A love her heart gave me the chance to find.

And that's the happiest ending I could ever ask for.

CHAPTER 7

The Girl with the Almond Eyes

I WAS FOURTEEN THE FIRST TIME I SAW HER.

She was standing beneath the awning outside our school's administration building, holding a green umbrella speckled with cartoon frogs. Her uniform was soaked at the hem, her shoes ruined by the heavy rain, but she looked like summer anyway.

She had long black hair, wind-kissed cheeks, and a smile like sunlight breaking through clouds.

She smiled at me, almost gently. Her almond eyes took in the soaked version of me like someone who actually mattered.

"You look like you need this," she said, offering me her umbrella, moving over to make room for me.

I didn't take it.

Instead, I memorized the shape of her fingers on the curved plastic handle, the way her wet hair clung to her cheek, the rhythm of her voice.

I wrote about her that night.

It was a poem, I realized later on. My first one.

She never knew.

Her name was Mireya.

She lived in a small white house with potted daisies on the windowsill, while I lived two blocks over, in a place that never smelled like anything but old rust and rain that never dries.

People called me Niko.

The boy with the busted life and even more busted shoes. My father was in prison. My mother didn't come home unless she had to; she lived in bingo halls and at mahjong tables instead.

I saw her every day in school. She liked to sit beneath the fire escape behind the cafeteria and read. Sometimes I pretended to smoke just so I could sit near her. She'd wrinkle her nose and say, "That'll kill you, you know."

I shrugged. "So will living."

She never laughed at that. She'd just glance at me with those almond eyes and say, "Don't make dying your ambition."

I didn't know how to tell her it already was.

I watched her from the corners of hallways, the back of classrooms I snuck into just to see her.

She always noticed people, even the invisible ones. She talked to me sometimes. She once gave me a stick of banana cue when I had nothing to eat. She even laughed at a joke I didn't mean to say out loud.

She was kind. Unshakably, stupidly kind.

Mireya didn't belong in my world.

But she lived in my poetry.

I started writing because of her. I hid my poems in notebooks and later, when I joined the gang, in scraps of receipt paper and cigarette boxes.

I never gave her one. I never had the guts. But I wrote like I was bleeding ink. Like every line might save me.

When we were seventeen, she gave me a Band-Aid. I had a broken lip and a bruised eye from a fight I didn't win, and she pressed it into my hand like it was a treasure.

"You don't have to keep doing this, Niko," she said.

But I did. For my brothers who were my only real family. For the streets of De la Rama. For the ones who would die if I didn't hold the line.

Life caught up with me, as it always does.

My father died in a riot at the provincial jail. My mother's lungs gave up on her and the cigarettes she loved more than me.

I didn't go to college. I joined the Marilas, made it a full-time job. Not because I wanted to. Because I had to. We were the ones who kept order at the docks. We were monsters, but we were family.

And still I wrote.

In ink and shadows, in blood and silence. I wrote her name in letters I never sent. Wrote apologies I could never give. Wrote confessions I never had the courage to say.

Wrote about another life, one where I could actually stand under the frog umbrella with the almond-eyed girl of my dreams.

She stayed in the city and became a nurse.

She always helped out in our neighborhood, smiling at those who came in pain, in need, and in desperation. Once, I saw her patch up a teenaged boy who got shot in a turf fight. No questions asked, even when she saw our colors.

She looked at me then.

"Niko," she said. "You look tired. Do you need anything?"

She spoke without fear. Without judgment.

I couldn't even answer.

I left before I did something stupid.

We crossed paths again and again. At the public market. A church pew. A wake for someone we both knew. She always said hi. I always froze.

My brothers laughed and said she was too good for me. I agreed.

But I wrote her another poem.

One night, I saw her in an all-hours coffee shop near the river. She wore her hair in a braid, and her white uniform was rumpled from what must have been a long shift.

I asked for two black coffees from the counter. I didn't realize my own hands were trembling as the barista handed me the change.

I went to the tiny two-seat table she had settled on outdoors.

"May I join you?" I asked as I put one of the red cardboard cups in front of her.

She looked up, not surprised at all to see me. She only nodded.

Her almond eyes took me in closely as I settled on the stool across hers.

"You look…" she began, but trailed off.

I waited.

"You still look tired, Niko."

I gave her a smile that didn't reach anything. "You remembered me. And my name."

"I remember everything."

I wanted to say it then, more than anything.

Then why didn't you see I was always yours?

But I didn't.

I finished my coffee without saying another word, but I left something on the table, in the space between our red cups.

It's one of my old poems written on the inside of a cigarette box.

She didn't say anything.

I didn't look back.

The war came fast.

Turf was turf. Blood was blood. De la Rama was ours, even if the Valientes didn't agree.

We lost three boys in one week.

I told myself I was doing it for the family. But in my darkest moments, when I stood in the rain with my hands still shaking from the blade or the gun or the weight of the choice, I thought of her.

The girl with the almond eyes who once told me to live.

I didn't expect the bullet. No one ever does.

It tore through my side like fire.

I bled out in the alley behind the videoke bar, beneath a flickering light and the eyes of the patron saint of voyages painted on the dock walls.

My phone buzzed once. It was a message I'd scheduled to send at nine in the evening.

To her.

Somehow, I knew tonight was going to be it.

The message just had three lines:

You were my sun.

You were the only thing that made me write.

I hope you smile when you think of me.

I closed my eyes thinking of her hands. Of the Band-Aid and the banana cue.

Of the green umbrella with the frogs.

Of the moments she always said my name like it meant

something more than just a boy life threw to the wind without a second thought.

I thought of her first words to me.

"You look like you need this."

This time, I answered. Because I knew this was my last chance.

Yes, Mireya. I need you.

I love you. I always will.

Maybe, in another life, I would have joined her under the umbrella, in the space she made for me.

Maybe, then, I would have made her mine.

But in this one...

She was the only poem I ever finished.

He dies on a Thursday.

I didn't understand the message I got from him that night, but I do now.

I find out on a Saturday, when a man with eyes like steel and tattoos like maps knocks on our gate at almost midnight.

He's terrifying, tall and built like a tank, wearing a nondescript black shirt and faded camouflage pants. He doesn't speak at first. He just stares at me.

Then he hands me a red reusable bag. As I take it with trembling hands, I hear pieces of paper and cardboard scrunching against each other.

"I'm Mart Marila," he says at last. "Niko's brother."

I nod, swallowing hard, too afraid to blink.

"He wrote these for you," he says, voice low, like it hurts to speak. He tilts his head at the bag. "We found them with his things."

He doesn't stay. He nods once and disappears into the night like a shadow.

I lock up and go inside the house. I sit on the sofa and pour out the bag's contents onto the low table.

Inside are poems. Dozens of them, maybe even more than a hundred. All scribbled onto torn cardboard packaging or oddly shaped sheets of paper.

Some of them are half-finished, some torn, all bleeding with longing. My name is in every one.

So is the name of the boy with the bruised knuckles and tired, sad eyes. The boy I always noticed. The boy I always wanted to save.

The boy I wanted to give my heart to, but never let me in.

I sit and read until the sun comes up.

I cry like I never cried before.

And when I finish the last one, I kiss the piece of cardboard, the one where Niko had doodled a girl with an umbrella surrounded by frogs and hearts.

I kiss the words he had written in red ink

You were my first warmth.

You were the only good thing I never touched, the dream I never deserved, the sun I watched rise from a rooftop, knowing I would always belong to the night.

I wrote you poems you'll never read.
You smiled at me like I wasn't lost.
You looked at me like I mattered.
I think that's what saved me for as long as it did.
And I'm sorry.
I'm sorry I couldn't be better. Sorry I never told you.
I wish I could see you one last time. I wish you could read this. I wish you could have known.
I loved you.
I loved you more than any of them will ever understand.
I hope you never forget to carry your umbrella.
It's raining again.
And I remember everything about you.
~ Niko

And I whisper into the bleeding dawn, "I remember everything, too, Niko."

CHAPTER 8

Flowers for the Dead

I DON'T KNOW HIS NAME.

But every time I pass the plaza near the old church, he's there. Always kneeling in the soil, sleeves rolled up, arms flecked with dirt, hands cradling blooms like they're made of glass. He moves like sunlight, warm and unhurried.

And whenever he sees me, he smiles.

That smile.

I'm supposed to avoid patterns. Routine breeds vulnerability. But I can't stop walking by the plaza since I moved to Arevalo.

Not when I know he'll be there. Not when I know, without fail, he'll leave a flower on the edge of the bench I always pass.

Today, it's a yellow-orange daisy. Bold and bright, almost defiant, against the cloudy day around me.

I pick it up, twirl the stem between my fingers, and keep walking.

I'm a killer.

It's what I do. What I was made for.

The men who raised me never gave me real names. Just contracts and an unbreakable professional code.

To them, I was never even a girl. Or a woman.

I'm just Max.

They carved instinct into my spine, turned emotion into static, and told me love was weakness. I believed them for years.

Then came him.

I don't know why I started watching him. Maybe it was the way he treated every flower like a miracle. Or the way he hummed to himself, off-key and soft.

No mask. No pretenses. Just…peace.

I don't know peace. I know orders, targets, and a hundred ways to make each kill look different from the others.

Still, I make time to pass by.

I reroute.I learn he comes every morning by six. I learn he doesn't use gloves because he says the flowers feel sadness when they're touched by something artificial.

One morning, he catches me watching.

"You always look so sad," he says. The gentleness in his voice hits me like a bullet.

I don't answer. I can't.

He kneels down and pulls a lily from a pallet. "This one's for you. It's for healing."

I stare at the glistening white petals. I don't take it.

He places it on the ground next to my feet before turning back to his work.

For the first time, I don't pick up the flower he gave me.

My latest target is someone important. Big businessman with lots of guards. The client is a politician who knows the businessman plans to run for the Congress spot of his district.

The job takes weeks to plan.

And when it goes wrong—when I underestimate their firepower, when the sirens come faster than I expected—I run.

I'm bleeding. My left side burns where the bullet grazed me.

There's nowhere to go. No safehouse close. No contact who won't ask questions.

Except him.

I stumble into the plaza, lungs screaming.

The sun is just rising, casting gold over everything.

And he's there.

He sees me right away. I hear the muffled sound of his spade hitting the dirt.

He rushes to my side, but couldn't reach me on time.

I collapse at his feet.

"Help," I rasp. "Please."

He doesn't ask any questions. He doesn't even say

anything. He just lifts me in his arms and carries me to the sidecar of his *pedicab.*

I hear him breathe a little heavier as he pedals away from the plaza.

His house smells like rosemary and soil. There are pots of aloe vera by the window and a bundle of roses on the table. He lays me on his sofa, working silently and efficiently.

He cleans the wound with surprising ease.

As he stitches me up, he says softly, "I'm Ronnie."

"Max," I answer.

Then I pass out.

When I wake, it's night.

He's sitting across from me, reading. When I move, he looks up.

There's no fear or anger or wariness on his face. Just… concern.

"You're lucky," he says. "That bullet could have ended you."

I try to sit up. Pain sears through me. "You should have left me."

He shrugs. "Didn't want to."

"You don't know me."

"I know enough. You're tired. You're alone and sad. And you're not as bad as you think."

He hands me a steaming cup of coffee.

"You could have gotten into trouble," I tell him.

He smiles. "But I didn't."

I stay. I don't mean to, but I do.

A week passes, then two. I sleep on his couch. I start helping him water the plants. He teaches me their names.

I find out he wanted to be a doctor and was even studying in college to be one. He'd dropped out on his third year to look after his sick mother, who ran a small flower garden that had been in her family for generations. His father, who died while he was still in high school, had worked for the church and the convent, doing maintenance and gardening. When his mother passed away five years ago, he simply took on the jobs they left behind.

One night, as I warily look at the rice cooking in the silver pot, I ask, "Why do you keep giving me flowers?"

He gives me a thoughtful look as he unwraps a small parcel of *liempo* he'd bought from the market. He now knows it's my favorite.

"Because you look like someone who's never been given anything just because," he answers, the words spoken a little too slowly and honestly for my liking.

I could only stare at him.

"And I like seeing your eyes soften," he adds. "You're beautiful, but the first time I gave you that pink rose, your eyes glowed like sunrise. Maybe that's why. You remind me of the light during sunrise."

We don't kiss until the night before I'm supposed to leave.

I haven't told him. I can't. I don't know what this is, what I'm allowed to feel.

But I break when he brushes a soil-stained hand on my cheek and whispers, "You don't have to go, Max."

So I kiss him.

It feels like everything I never let myself want.

That night, we don't sleep.

That night, I let myself believe.

That I could want something, and be wanted back.

But I know—the world isn't soft.

It's a harsh, judgmental bastard, just like the men who created me.

My past catches up.

They find me in my safehouse near the mangrove reserve.

They tell me to finish the contract. One last target. One last loose end.

After this, they promise me I could leave. Or live. Depends on who says what, really.

I tell them to stuff the money up their asses. I tell them we're quits once the job is done.

But that night, I bleed again.

This time, it's so much worse.

But I remember the light in his eyes, the stains on his hands, the warmth of his lips.

So I go back to the plaza at sunrise.

One last time

But no one's there.

I collapse on the bench where he left me flowers.

I can't breathe. Everything hurts.

I close my eyes.

Then…

I feel him.

Arms lifting me.

His voice sounds distant, panicked. "No. No, no, no. You don't get to leave me now."

I try to smile. "You're here. You're finally here."

He cries.

As the world begins to turn black, I say the words.

"Thanks, Ronnie. Love you."

I wake to sun through linen curtains.

To the smell of roses and lilies on the table.

My body hurts, but I'm alive.

He's asleep beside the sofa, bundled in a thin blanket on a mat on the floor next to me. There's dried dirt on the hem of his pants and dark circles under his eyes.

I reach for his soil-stained hand.

"Ronnie?"

He stirs.

His eyes flutter open, then a smile spreads across his face.

"You stayed," I say.

"I told you," he answers. "You're not alone."

He stands up and takes something from the table.

He sinks to his knees before me, and hands me a bright, bold, and defiant daisy.

"I don't think I want to be alone anymore," I tell him.

He nods, then kisses me.

I kiss him back.

"Then you'll never be," he murmurs against my lips.

And for the first time, I believe I'm allowed to stay.

CHAPTER 9

The Hotel Room

THERE HE IS.

I don't expect him to be there when I open the door.

But he proves me wrong.

I don't ask why he chooses to meet in the same hotel I do. Maybe it's coincidence. Maybe it's fate, or maybe fate is just another word for good timing but with all the wrong reasons.

He leans against the doorframe as if he belongs to the twilight, all shadows and half-hooded eyelids. He smells like cigarette smoke, wearing the same dark blue jacket from years ago.

He doesn't look at me right away.

And I remember the first time I saw him, all those years ago. I was his supervisor at the insurance company and he'd been an encoder. He'd been the fastest to meet quotas in my team, but he never said much to anyone. After a month, he started waiting for me to finish work, then waited until I got into my taxi. He even asked me to text him once I reached home.

Months later, he got into the taxi with me. I took him to a motel.

Then I moved to a government office in Manila.

"You're late," I tell him.

"You aren't supposed to be here," he replies, finally meeting my eyes. "What will they say about their golden girl sneaking around?"

I shake my head, a little tiredly. "And yet here we are."

"Here we are," he echoes, giving me a smile.

It's lopsided, weary, familiar. God, it's familiar.

It's always like this with us. Half-smiles. Half-truths. Half-promises. All of them crumbling at the edges.

The door clicks shut behind him. The rain outside is a distant hush against the windowpane. He shrugs off his damp jacket, tosses it onto the armchair like he owns the room, like he owns this silence between us. But he doesn't. He never did.

The room is quiet except for the hum of the city below. Floor-to-ceiling windows show a skyline we both once dreamed of conquering.

"This is a big change," he says softly, leaning against the wall, watching me, his eyes tracing every movement like he hasn't forgotten a thing. "The room's clean, for a start. Surprised you said you're going to foot the bill. My baby girl can afford better now, can't she? "

I scowl at him. I got the room at a discount using the Undersecretary's name, but I don't want to give him the satisfaction of being right.

"Don't call me that," I bite out instead. "I'm not your baby. And I'm definitely not a girl."

He frowns down at me. "You'll always be to me, Lee."

I shake my head, then sit at the table and pour a glass of red wine.

"Fancy," he murmurs.

I incline my head in casual agreement, as if I didn't book this hotel because of him. As if we didn't always end up together, somehow, when the world got too complicated and we ran out of excuses not to forget.

At least for a while.

He doesn't ask for a drink, but I pour for him too. Old habits, I guess.

We used to drink light beer and eat fried chicken, after the motel.

"I thought you would appreciate something…different," I say.

He smiles.

But I know he doesn't do different. He'd self-destructed weeks after I left my old workplace. By the time I'd heard about it from practically everyone at the insurance company, I was already far away from Iloilo.

"How long are you gonna be in town for?" he asks, sliding into the seat across mine. The soft light of the room cast half his face in eerie, distorted shadow.

"Just the night," I answer. "I'm flying back to work tomorrow evening. I told my boss I'm visiting my parents."

He lifts his glass to me in a mock toast. "Clever girl."

I don't answer, choosing instead to let the word go. I take a sip of my wine, not looking at him but at the bed before us.

"So why now?" he asks softly. "Why this room, this night?"

I sigh. "I know what happened. What you did when I left. You shouldn't have done that."

"What did I do?" he challenges me, almost immediately.

"You didn't listen to anyone. You completely and utterly disregarded all authority by nearly killing Doc Simeon. You're lucky they didn't have you arrested."

He slams the glass down, wine sloshing all over the polished wood. Then he jumps to his feet.

"I didn't come here for this bullshit," he says. "I came for you."

In the dim light, I can see his shoulders shaking, but his voice sounds steady.

"I know," I answer softly.

I put my own glass down and stand, blocking his way.

"That's why I'm here. I want to ask you to stop whatever it is you're doing before you can't anymore."

He shakes his head. "I can't, Lee. You know I can't."

"Dennis." His name escapes my lips, an apology he never asked for. An apology I could never say out loud.

He winces at the sound—and there it is.

That knife-twist in my chest. The one I thought I'd buried under logic and time.

The familiar, breathless tightness whenever I look into his deep-set eyes, so dark they're almost black.

I miss him.

"I love you, Lee," he says. "I loved you the moment you told the VP you could put me to work. You never judged. You just believed."

The pain reaches my stomach, making me feel deathly cold.

Love.

He still loves me.

But I don't say it back.

"I still believe," I say cautiously. "And I never judged you. I knew you were better than everyone else, even if you didn't finish college. I never looked at what you had on paper."

He freezes, his body wound tight like a rubber band ready to snap.

"I looked at you," I continue. "I still see you. I still see the man who promised me he won't let me down."

"I promised you," he retorts icily. "I didn't promise any of them. When Simeon questioned my work, I told him to fuck off and retire. He shouted at me, made everyone hear that I was a dropout who couldn't even meet quota. So I broke his nose. People forget I used to be good at Silat."

I sigh impatiently. "Christ."

"It was never the same without you, baby girl," he says, softer now. "It all got fucked up so quickly. I didn't even realize I was already fired. I was just too…mad."

"At me," I offer.

He shakes his head. "No. At the world. At them. Never at you."

That does it.

I put my arms around him. His heartbeat thunders in my ear.

"Don't go then," I say. "Stay. Stay the night."

"Say it then," he mutters into my hair. "Just say it, Lee."

I take a deep breath.

"I love you, Dennis." And I just couldn't stop there. "I miss you. I don't why, but it's not the same without you."

He doesn't answer right away. He doesn't even move an inch.

"You should have just told me the minute I walked through that door," he finally says. His eyes take me in, up and down, lips to throat, chest to forehead.

I shake my head and step back, but he reaches for me, hands sliding around my waist.

"I wanted to make sure you're still not completely insane," I shoot back. "I heard stories. Not so flattering ones, I'm afraid."

He laughs then. That low, familiar sound that vibrates through me like a memory I could never shake.

I sit on the edge of the bed. He joins me a beat later.

We're not touching, but the space between us is electric.

"So," I say, "do you want to talk about it?"

He doesn't say anything in response. He just looks at me like he's memorizing every inch of me all over again. I can see it in his eyes.

"Do you remember the first time?" he asks instead.

"The motel in Molo? Or us?"

"Both."

I close my eyes. I remember the rain. I stayed back at the office to sign hundreds of new membership cards. I remember the feel of his hand around mine as he slid into the taxi next to me.

The way he asked me, "Do you want to forget everything for a while?"

It felt like a lifetime ago.

"You made me feel like flying," I say, smiling a bit.

Now, he touches my hand, lightly. "You said you didn't believe in forever. You said you believe in seizing the moment."

"And you said you didn't believe in anything at all."

We both lie sometimes.

He doesn't answer. Not with words.

He moves closer. His hands slide into my hair, and mine find his chest.

"Tell me to stop, Lee," he breathes.

"I can't."

And I don't.

The clothes come off in pieces, peeling away the years between us. Our touches feel like confessions we could never say.

It's like no time has passed at all. His hands know the slope of my hips. My mouth remembers the taste of his name. We fall back into each other like drowning people finding air.

The night is slow, lingering, beautiful. We spend it tangled in the thick white sheets. Fingers skimming skin. Kisses that ask questions, ones answered only in gasps and caresses.

When he whispers my name, tells me he missed *us*, I wonder if he feels it too—the pain of something lost and almost found again.

We don't promise anything.

But we say *I love you.*

Because in this hotel room, that is the most real thing in the world.

We don't sleep.

Morning comes quietly. The light is gentle as it skims over my skin, filtering in small ripples through the blinds.

He holds me close and says, "This doesn't change anything."

"I know," I answer. "At least I tried."

But we both feel it. That thing in the air. That almost that always threatens to become more, if only we let it.

He kisses me squarely on the mouth.

"I think that's why I love you," he murmurs against my lips. "And that's why you'll leave."

A lone tear slides down my cheek. He brushes it away with the back of his hand, exhaling softly.

"Promise me you'll do better," I tell him. "Just try. Not for me. For you. You deserve more than what you're doing to yourself."

He pulls me closer, his fingers running through my hair.

"I already had more," he says. "I had you."

The dam finally breaks.

I spend the sunrise crying in his arms.

He doesn't say anything. He just keeps holding me, soothing my tears with soft kisses and feather-light touches.

The last thing I remember is seeing his skinned knuckles, his callused palms, as his fingers trace the gentlest lines down my cheeks.

"Goodbye, Dennis," I say softly, dreamily, before drifting off to an exhausted sleep.

The room is bright when I wake up.

I check the time on my phone, then stare at the ceiling. I know before I look around the room.

He's gone.

A note sits on the nightstand in his handwriting.

Still blocky, a little too sharp. Just like him.

Thank you for the night. You'll always be my baby girl.

I trace the words, the same way I traced the hard, sullen lines of his face.

And in the quiet between heartbeats, in the space where the tears and the ache should be, I realize something.

We never made promises.

But love doesn't need those to leave a mark.

It just needs one night.

CHAPTER 10

Memory of Rain

THE RAIN COMES FAST, THE WAY IT ALWAYS DOES HERE. One moment the sky is swollen, thick with warning. The next, it just…gives up.

And then everything falls.

The first drops are loud and angry, smacking the pavement in uneven bursts. Within seconds, it's a full downpour, merciless and unapologetically loud.

Umbrellas snap. Drivers swerve to the curb. The street clears as if it's been evacuated by some silent order.

But I don't move.

I just stand back, leaning against the brick wall of this old café I haven't stepped inside in years. It's still the same— the little awning that sags in the middle, the smell of burnt espresso, the familiar pastries inside the glass display.

The awning provides little to no protection from the gusts of water and wind. My shirt clings to my back. My hair's dripping into my eyes. And still, I stay rooted to the spot.

I don't know why I came here. This place is for the

younger crowd, with so many colleges scattered from block to block.

Maybe it's habit. Or a twinge of memory, made of endless nights and cruel mornings. Or maybe it's just the kind of place you end up in when you're lost and don't want to admit it.

Then I hear her.

Not her voice. Her steps.

I don't know how I recognize them after all this time, but I do. The click of heels against the slick pavement. The sudden half-stumble. The curse under her breath. It all hits me at once, familiar and alive.

I turn my head.

And there she is.

She's soaked to the bone, skirt heavy and clinging around her legs, hair plastered to her cheeks. She's giggling breathlessly as if she just outran the whole storm. She ducks under the awning and stops cold the moment she sees me.

Her eyes lock with mine. The light isn't much, but it's enough for me to see the flash of recognition in them.

My throat tightens. My hands go numb.

Because it's her.

Older now, sure. But still her. Still the same laugh, the same eyes.

And just like that, I'm twenty again.

Wild and in love and convinced we were made to survive anything.

She stares like I'm a ghost.

I offer a smile, just a small one. The kind I used to give her across the table when we were pretending to study, or when I'd sneak my fingers across her thigh under the dining table at her parents' house.

"Hi, Vanessa," I say.

It barely makes it out of my mouth.

She blinks hard, her lips parting before sound actually comes out. "Jerry. Hi."

The sound of my name splinters something in me I thought I buried a long time ago.

We stand there for a moment in the kind of silence that doesn't ask to be filled. The rain rages around us, but inside this little pocket of space, time bends. It tries to remember.

She doesn't say anything more. Neither do I. But I feel her beside me, close enough that I can sense the warmth radiating off her skin. Her scent cuts through the rain. Vanilla and something soft and fresh.

She still smells the same. She even wears her bag the same way, slung across her body like a sash.

Finally, I speak.

"You still hate the rain?"

She lets out a quiet laugh, shaking her head. "You still love it?"

"Always."

My grin flashes without thinking. The kind of grin I only ever wore with her.

She looks away before I can hold her gaze.

Smart girl.

Because I would have kept looking.

And I know she remembers too.

The same storm. The same street. Her arms around me on the back of my motorbike, her voice shrill in my ear, calling me a lunatic as we tore through flooded roads. The way I pulled her under this awning, many storms ago.

How I kissed her with water spilling over us like we were drowning and on fire at the same time. Her laughter against my mouth. Her fingers in my hair. The rain tasting like salt and the promise of being invincible.

I remember it all.

I remember the last time we saw each other too.

The fight.

The things we said. The things we didn't.

I remember how I left. And how she didn't stop me.

Thunder rips across the sky. She flinches, just slightly. But I could still feel it, after all this time.

My fingers twitch. I want to reach for her. God, I want to.

But I don't.

Because what if she doesn't want me to?

What if that one move breaks whatever fragile truce we're standing in now?

So I keep my hands at my sides, like a coward. Or a man who's already lost her once.

The rain eventually eases. It becomes a whisper instead of a shout.

She turns to me, and her voice is softer than anything I've ever heard. "I should go."

I nod. I don't trust myself to speak.

She glances up and down the street, then takes a step. And another.

The words leave my mouth before I can stop them. "Come on. I'll take you."

She looks at me over her shoulder, raising a brow. "You still have the bike?"

I glance toward the curb. "Always."

She hesitates, just for a second. Then she nods.

I walk to the bike and pull the spare helmet from my pack, holding it out to her. It's scuffed, but still solid. It's the same one she's always used. I kept it all this time, even when I told myself I had thrown everything about her away.

Her fingers graze the surface like she's touching glass. She says nothing.

I help her into the old raincoat from under the seat. It's too big now, or maybe she just feels smaller. But I wrap it around her anyway, button it at her throat. My hands brush her collarbone. She doesn't react; she only looks at me, her eyes a little wide.

We don't speak as we ride.

Her arms go around me, loose and hesitant at first. But then she relaxes as we speed down the highway.

For a moment, it's as if no time had passed. As if we're still the same two people who broke curfews and kissed in alleyways and believed love could outrun destruction.

But I don't take the long way like I used to.

I head straight for the subdivision and stop at her gate.

The engine quiets graciously. Silence falls between us like an umbrella.

She climbs off slowly. She pulls the helmet from her head. Her hair clings to her face and neck.

She turns to me, holding the helmet out.

I take it back.

Then she hesitates, her hands reaching for the lapels of the raincoat.

"Keep it," I say softly.

Her eyes lift to mine. "Why?"

I shrug. "Just…keep it. In case it rains again."

She doesn't answer.

But she leans in.

And presses a kiss to my cheek.

It's not the kind of kiss that wants more. It's not a promise. Not a beginning.

It's a memory. Soft and grateful, but still broken.

"Thank you," she says against my jaw.

I nod, but I can't speak.

She walks to the door.

I swallow, hard. "Hey, Vanessa."

She pauses and turns to face me once more. "Yes?"

"You know where to find me," I say. "Whenever you need a ride. No questions."

She smiles, but it looks like goodbye.

"That's sweet," she says. "I'll keep that in mind."

"Good."

I watch her walk toward the front door. Just as she

reaches it, she pauses. One hand on the knob, one still wrapped in the coat.

She turns slightly and raises a hand in a wave.

It's enough to say without speaking—*I remember.*

Then she slips inside.

And I sit there in the silence after the rain, helmet in my lap, the scent of her still on my jacket and my skin.

It's not the storm that stays with me.

It's her kiss.

Her silence.

And the raincoat I'll never get back.

The one she'll wear when it rains.

The one she'll wear thinking of the boy who will always give her a ride to everywhere and nowhere.

As I rev the engine and ride off, between the downpour and the past and the pieces of us that never quite fit back together, I almost believe in us again.

In the impossible yet echoing hope between heartbeats.

And I wonder if she still felt it too.

CHAPTER 11

One Last Song

THE MUSIC STARTS SLOW.

Just a few notes, plucked gently. The kind of beginning that aches.

I don't even realize I'm holding my breath until the first line slips through the mic, low and worn like the soles of a favorite pair of sneakers.

"Didn't think I'd see you again," he says—sings, rather—but it feels like both.

I sit in the farthest booth of this quiet little bar, head and shoulders hunched, trying to blend into the shadows.

It's not a crowded place, and that's why I chose it. It was always his kind of scene.

But I didn't expect him to actually be here. Not on open mic night.

Not after all these years.

And yet, there he is.

Cal is older now, but still him. Still all long fingers and lean strength, unruly hair, that worn leather strap across his shoulder anchoring the guitar to his body like a second skin. He used to say it was the only thing that held him together.

The first time we met, we were seventeen. I had braces. He had calluses and restlessness. We shared a setlist and a single cracked earbud between us, passing it back and forth like communion.

I became the voice. He became the strings.

For two years, we played every local gig we could find. Birthday parties, art fairs, weddings, beachfront dives. He wrote the songs, I sang them.

We swore to each other we'd move to Manila. Record something real. Chase the dream together. Maybe even get our own album.

But then life happened.

My parents split.

His dad got sick.

I got a scholarship in another city.

He stayed.

We stopped calling.

It wasn't dramatic. Not really. There was no big fight, no slammed doors or cruel words. Just silence that stretched too long. Empty inboxes. Unsent messages. The slow fadeout of a love too young to fight the noise of the world.

And yet, I still hear his music in my dreams.

And now, after ten years, here he is onstage. Singing what can only be a new song, with every lyric a knife.

"You wore stars in your eyes, And I swore I'd give you the sky. But I stayed down here, And watched you fly."

I press my hand over my mouth.

My heart is thundering so loudly I'm afraid the whole bar can hear it. He hasn't looked up. Not once. His gaze is pinned to the strings, fingers moving with the kind of elegance that only comes from pain and time.

"You lit the fire, I fanned the flame, But only one of us got a name. You sang the chorus, I stayed behind the frame."

I remember that line—or something close to it. Back when we were writing songs in his garage, surrounded by empty Coke bottles and mosquito coils. He used to hum while I paced. He used to say he didn't have the voice for the stage, that he liked being the echo and not the roar.

But he was wrong. He's the whole damn storm.

The song ends with a single, trembling note. A heartbeat held between thumb and forefinger.

When he lets it go, the silence that follows cracks my chest wide open.

There's scattered applause and a few appreciative whistles. The people in front nod and smile at him.

Cal dips his head and murmurs a soft, "Thanks, guys."

The lights go up, and he begins packing his guitar.

I know I should leave, but I don't.

Because some part of me knows this is the last chance.

I get to my feet. The floor creaks beneath me as I cross

the room. Cal's back is still turned. I watch his shoulders tense as I approach.

"That was beautiful," I say.

His hand freezes on the strap. Slowly, he turns. Then his eyes, warm and dark as a rainy night, find mine.

He doesn't speak for a long time. Just looks at me.

"Astra," he finally says.

My name on his lips is enough to send a chill down my spine.

"Hey, Cal."

"You came."

I smile faintly. "Didn't know you'd be here."

He lets out a soft laugh, but there's no humor in it. "Neither did I."

I tilt my head. "Open mic night, huh?"

"First one in years."

I step closer, touching his forearm for the first time in years. "That song. It was about me."

He looks down. "They're all about you."

My breath catches.

He picks up his guitar case and gestures to an empty table near the back of the bar.

We settle on the chairs quietly. A waiter brings over two ice-cold bottles of light beer.

As I sip my drink, I look at Cal. I can read very little from his face. He's always been good at hiding what he thinks, how he feels.

There's so much I want to ask. So many things we left unsaid.

"I thought you'd forget me," I say. "After everything."

"I tried," he admits. "But you don't forget the person who taught you how to feel."

My hand tightens around the beer bottle, but I force out the words, trying to sound casual.

"What happened to the studio plans? The Manila dream?"

He shrugs. "My dad got worse. I couldn't leave. And then…I guess I convinced myself you didn't need me."

"I always did."

He shakes his head, taking a sip of his beer before he speaks. "You never called."

"Neither did you."

"I didn't want to hold you back, Astra."

"You were never the thing holding me back. You were the reason I even dared to go."

We both look away.

We don't say anything for nearly half a song that plays on the bar speakers.

Then he says softly, "I still write songs. Even if no one listens."

"I still sing," I offer. "Alone, for the most part. In the car. Or in the shower. I kind of got a thing for K-pop now."

He laughs. "Still the same voice?"

I smile back. "Little raspier now. More rock than pop, if you will."

"Still. I'd like to hear it again."

A beat of silence stretches between us.

Then I break it. "I have to leave tomorrow. Back to Singapore. I just came home for a week. It's the longest time off I could get."

"Figures. It's that same media company, right? It's gotten kind of big now, I heard. Correct me if I'm wrong."

"It's gotten kind of busier," I say honestly. "Singapore moves differently."

He nods slowly. "If you say so. It's just me and the shop now. My mom couldn't hold on after dad passed."

I move closer, then squeeze his hand. It's a world of stories on its own. It's bigger now, a little harder and rougher than I remember.

"I'm so sorry, Cal. You should have told me. Emailed or something. I could have—"

"No," he cuts me off gently. "Don't. It's okay. You were living your life."

"Doesn't mean you're not in it."

His hand covers mine, squeezes back.

"Astra…" His voice trails off, but his eyes tell me everything.

I nod. "We can still be…us, right? Even if just for tonight. We owe each other that."

His eyes search mine. Then he stands.

"Let's go home," he says, picking up his guitar case with one hand, holding out the other to me.

I don't think. I just take it.

He still lives in the same place, a small, sturdy two-story built next to his family's auto repair shop.

We end up in the same place where we used to make music. He still has the same record player and the stack of vinyls he'd collected from his grandfather, father, and uncle.

An old photo of us—from our first performance as a duo during the acquaintance party—hangs on the wall next to the stereo cabinet.

We don't speak much. We don't need to.

We share instant noodles and slightly stale *teren-teren* bread.

Afterward, he plays our old songs. I sing in my new raspier voice, which he tells me reminds him of Meredith Brooks.

And when the music ends, we don't.

We kiss like we're still seventeen. Like time hasn't scarred us, and the world didn't win.

We fall into his bed like it's our stage, and the curtain has finally dropped.

He holds me like a lifeline.

I hold him like a promise I never stopped meaning.

In the morning, the sun spills through the thin, graying curtains. I'm wrapped in his arms, head on his chest.

His fingers draw circles on my back. And I think, no. He's writing music on me. He always does.

"Stay," he says.

And for one, perfect, suspended moment, I almost say yes.

But life calls. Work. Responsibilities. Realities we can't undo.

I rise, dressing slowly. I move around the room as if I'm in a dream I don't want to end.

He watches me closely.

At the door, I turn.

"I meant what I said. About still needing you."

He nods. "I know."

"Maybe…someday?"

He smiles, but it doesn't reach his eyes. "Maybe."

I pick up my bag and leave.

The door clicks shut.

As I make way back to the street of his village, back to my parents' house, and back to the perfect, sterile streets and buildings of Singapore, our songs still play in my head.

They always will.

CHAPTER 12

A Dance of Years

THE GYM SMELLS LIKE SWEAT, SUGAR, AND TOO MANY what-ifs.

My heels ache from my cheap shoes. My makeup is running. There's a rip in the hem of my dress I didn't notice until I sat down after the last slow song.

Everyone's still here, lingering past midnight like they don't want it to end. The party is quiet now. There's less shouting, but more laughter softened by goodbyes. The kind of hush that comes when all the pretending, glitter, and adrenaline fade.

And that's when I see him.

He stands near the exit, half in shadow. He looks like he's waiting for something. Or maybe someone.

He's wearing a blazer that's clearly not his, too big at the shoulders, wrinkled like it's lived three lives. His hair's pure chaos.

But he looks like the most beautiful mess I've ever seen.

He sees me before I say a word.

Of course he does.

He always does.

"Hey," I say softly.

"Hey," he answers.

He gives me a smile. I think I'm the only one who's ever seen it on his face.

We've been us since Grade Two. Since scraped knees and playground alliances and snacks traded at lunch. Since he showed me how to climb trees and get down like a final boss. Since I taught him how to lie convincingly to keep from being suspended for tardiness. Since we started pretending to be characters in our own secret stories.

And somewhere along the way, something stopped being pretend.

But we never talk about the thing we never talk about.

He nods toward me, as if he's trying to find the right words and settling on the simplest. "You looked nice tonight."

I snort, too tired to be flattered. "You mean this disco-ball disaster dress or the frizz halo on my head that breaks the laws of gravity?"

He doesn't find this funny.

"I mean you," he says, scowling.

I forget how to breathe.

Because he's not joking, or even teasing. He's just telling the truth.

I take a step forward, and he doesn't move.

The space between us shrinks, and suddenly everything feels tight—my chest, my throat, the string that's been stretched between us since forever. Tonight it pulls tighter, humming like it might snap or sing.

Someone at the DJ's table plays that last song again.

The slow one. The one we never danced to.

Avril Lavigne's 'I'm With You.'

I glance toward the center of the gym, where couples sway in uneven rhythms.

But I don't move. Neither does he. We just stand here, breathing in the shadow of the quiet we share.

"Do you remember," I murmur, "last summer we got caught in the rain? You gave me your jacket even though you were soaked through and shivering."

He nods. "You never gave it back."

I smile. "Still smells like you."

He smiles back, but it looks like it's breaking something in him to do it. "Is that…a good thing?"

I don't answer. Not with words, at least.

Instead, I reach out, barely. Just enough for my fingers to brush his.

He flinches. It's a ghost of a movement, but I see it.

But slowly, his hand turns, then his fingers hook through mine.

It's not something that screams.

It's a maybe. It's everything and nothing all at once.

It's enough to make my heart ache.

"Aidan," someone calls out into the dark.

We both look.

It's his brother, leaning out the car window, headlights flaring through the gym doors.

"You should go," I say.

And he does what he always does.

He lets go first.

"Goodnight, Raya."

Then he's gone.

We don't speak much after that.

Life does what life always does.

It pulls. It tears. It scatters.

We end up in different cities. In different time zones. With different jobs and different people.

But I still see his name in the corners of my screen.

He likes my photos on socials sometimes. I heart his throwback and nostalgic posts, the ones with song lyrics in the captions. He sends a meme on my birthday that makes me laugh harder than it should. I send him a playlist once, the same one he made me listen to when we danced in the kitchen that one afternoon we were supposed to make spaghetti for our class Christmas party.

We almost call. Almost message. Almost say it.

But we never talk about the thing we never talk about.

Still, when it rains, I reach for that jacket. Still tucked in the back of my closet, still stitched with memories of the boy who waits in the shadows but lets go first.

When I walk through crowded places, I look for messy hair and a blazer that never quite fits.

When I laugh too hard at something, I wonder if he'd find it funny too.

We were never a love story.

Not in the way people write them, or movies make us believe them to be.

We were a feeling. A moment in pockets of time.

A dance that we never had.

But this story stays with me anyway.

Tonight, there's a wedding at the fanciest resort in town.

They used to be our classmates. They both made it in Dubai and came back home to get married.

There are fairy lights everywhere. Music from the live band floats like glitter and dust in the wind. I'm heading to my car after exchanging greetings and goodbyes when I hear it.

The last song.

That song.

The one from the dance.

I'm With You.

It pulls me back to the ballroom like gravity.

I pause at the doorway, watching the bride and groom slow dance. Other couples are swaying on the dance floor. The singer does a great job at singing in Avril's style.

And my body feels hot and cold at the same time.

That's when I see him.

He's standing by the edge of the crowd, half in shadow. Just watching.

He looks older, broader. Tired in a way that feels achingly familiar.

But it's Aidan.

It's him.

Time stops, or maybe my heart does. Or maybe the world just decided to be kind for once.

Across the room, we lock eyes.

I don't know who moves first.

Maybe it's both of us.

Maybe it's always been both of us, just waiting for the right moment to step forward.

When we meet in the middle of the dance floor, I don't say anything.

He doesn't either.

He just holds out his hand.

This time, I take it.

This time, we don't almost.

This time, we dance all the way through.

And he never lets me go.

CHAPTER 13

The Wedding Guest

THE FIRST TIME I SEE HER AGAIN, SHE'S WRAPPED IN ivory lace, her arm hooked around the man she chose instead of me.

It's her wedding.

And I'm a guest. Just another name on the list.

But she looks at me.

She looks at me the same way she did the night before we broke.

She looks at me like I'm the only thing she wants to run to.

The music plays. The late afternoon sun shines over the glossy white sand of the five-star resort. People clap and cheer.

The air is thick with salt—tears and sea and unspoken apologies. The wedding is by the shore, where white chairs dot the sand like bones. Her veil dances in the wind. She laughs too loudly at the best man's speech. Her mother keeps dabbing at her eyes, saying how proud she is.

I sip wine and bubbly and watch her from behind my sunglasses, the same way I always did since we were teenagers.

Only steps behind, but never close enough.

My name isn't mentioned in any speeches. It shouldn't be.

The people who do recognize me treat me with polite curiosity, discussing the weather or my trip from Manila or my latest investigative piece.

But she glances my way when she thinks no one's looking. And the way she squeezes the groom's hand like she's bracing for something tells me she still remembers everything.

The way I would buy her only baby's breath because that's all that's left in the market after work.

The long nights reading and making love.

The lazy mornings drinking coffee and watching CNN and BBC on cable.

The final fight. The ache that never stopped.

She said she needed stability, predictability. I was stories and secrets and late-night flights.

He was steady and practical; a successful architect who practically designed half the new trade zone in the outskirts of our city. The kind of man one marries.

I told her I hoped she'd be happy. She told me to never come back.

So I left.

And she waited three years to say "I do."

They slow dance under the fairy lights, in the giant

gazebo decorated with light purple and pink flowers. Her cheek rests against his.

Still, her eyes find mine over his shoulder.

She doesn't cry. She's better than that. But her lips part as if she wants to tell me something.

I nod, just once. It's an answer.

But I know it's also a goodbye.

Later, when the guests are drunk and the tide is low, I find her barefoot at the deck of the resort, staring at the moonlight pooling on the slats of wood as waves roll underneath.

"You shouldn't be here," she says, not looking up.

"I wasn't going to stay."

"Why did you come?"

"Because you sent the invitation."

"I didn't think you'd say yes."

"You wanted me to."

She turns to me then.

Her cheeks are flushed. Her makeup has smudged at the corners. Her lips are trembling.

"You left."

"You asked me to."

"I thought it would hurt less."

"Did it?"

She doesn't answer.

I take a step forward. She doesn't move.

"You look beautiful, Elsie," I say. And I mean it. God, I mean it.

"Not for you."

"No." I smile at her, hoping she sees the way I've always seen her. "But you always were."

She takes a deep breath, like she knows she might drown.

"I waited for you, Gabe."

The words leave her like ripples of foam.

She continues. It sounds like a song. "Every birthday. Every New Year. Every first rain after the summer. I waited until it made me sick."

I nod slowly. "I know."

"And you didn't come."

There's no accusation in it. Only acceptance.

"I wanted you to live. I wanted you to have what you wanted."

"I did." Her smile is so broken I almost drop to my knees. "Just not the life I needed."

Silence follows. Around us, the tide ebbs and flows. I know it will change again soon.

"I should go," I say.

She nods, but she still doesn't move.

"Tell me you don't love me, Elsie. Give me something."

She looks at me, lips parting. Then she closes her mouth tightly. Tears brim from her eyes.

"I can't."

I nod, but I feel the tears in mine too.

I let them fall. Let her see them. If she can't give me something, I will.

I pull out a tiny bundle of baby's breath from my jacket and place it by her feet.

And I leave.

It rains as I make my way to the parking lot.

The kind of rain that tastes like ash and dust.

I stand alone as it crashes down on me, ruining my good suit.

I imagine her inside, staring at her reflection in the hotel mirror, maybe holding the flowers only the two of us understand, wondering if she'll survive this choice.

I hope she does.

This is what she wanted.

And I gave it all to her.

Because some people we love so much we let them go.

Tonight, the sky tells a story of two broken hearts still beating for each other.

And I was her last story.

Even if she'll never tell that story again.

Years later, I hear from a mutual friend that her marriage didn't last.

No scandals or fights. Just a quiet, aching unraveling.

She moved to her father's hometown. She teaches English and Journalism at the university there.

She lives near the sea, keeps to herself.

Every year, on her birthday, someone leaves an unmarked bundle of baby's breath at her gate.

She never asks who. She just keeps it in a glass of water until it fades and falls apart.

Then she waits for the next one.

CHAPTER 14

Mist and Blood

THE GRAY BUILDING APPEARS AT THE EDGE OF THE shore.

The mist parts, and I see what they call 'the dojo.'

There's no sign, no path.

There is nothing to attract or welcome students.

The place just…exists.

I first heard about it from an old woman who sold me Indian mangoes at the market. She took one glance at the bruise on my cheek and told me to find "the house where the Master lives."

Apparently, he'll teach me to dish it out just as well as I take it.

The other people at the market say the house has always been here, crouched like a waiting beast between the wet trees and the rocks that cradle the sea.

You don't find it on maps. You don't stumble into it by accident. You arrive when you have nowhere else to go.

I arrive on a Monday.

At least, I think it's Monday, because I'm wearing my school uniform.

My shoes are almost ripped in half. My lip is split from a fight I didn't win. My breath comes shallow, most likely from a bruised rib. My stomach's hollow, but my eyes burn. My wrists are a map of old bruises—some that faded into memory, others still pulsing beneath the skin.

I walk through the early morning fog, my arms wrapped around myself—not for warmth, but for armor. The plain gray walls rise out of the mist like something ancient. The roof is heavy with leaves. The courtyard pools with rain.

And the Master is there.

I don't know his name.

He looks like stone carved into a man—angular face, high cheekbones, narrow jaw, eyes that look like the mist I just walked through. His hair is long and black streaked with silver, tied back like a warrior from a forgotten time.

He watches me. I don't know if he's being kind or cruel or curious.

He's just still.

He even doesn't ask why I'm here.

He just picks up my soiled green backpack full of torn clothes and walks into the dojo.

And I follow.

I learn and serve in silence.

No formal greetings. No initiations. Just days that become weeks that become months.

I don't go to school, but I read the books that fill the shelves in the hallway.

I cook and clean and do laundry. I go to the market in town. He gives me money to buy supplies and pay bills.

I talk to the students and their parents like a model employee.

I sleep in a tiny outhouse at the edge of the property, nestled between groves of coconut trees.

The rest of the time I don't stop training.

He never raises his voice. He doesn't praise or scold.

He exists like gravity. Something I adjust to, something I resist. Something I eventually learn to trust.

When I stumble, he catches me.

When I scream, he lets me.

When I collapse, he waits.

When I get the attacks in the middle of the night, he carries me to the dojo and lets me cry myself to sleep on the mats.

I learn to move with precision. To strike without hesitation. To still my breath until even the rain sounds like rhythm. My fists learn to break brick. My muscles harden. My fire refines itself, no longer wild, but contained and ready.

And at night in my tiny outhouse, my heart racing with echoes of old horrors, I feel him there.

Something near enough to reach.

The year's typhoon season is the most cruel yet.

The sea winds grow vicious. My bones ache, but I still train in the courtyard barefoot, under the lashing rain, letting the cold needles bite me into clarity.

He passes me sometimes. Our eyes meet, but there are no words.

I've come to crave that between us.

One night, it all changes.

I'm walking back from town, a bag of supplies slung over my shoulder, when I see a figure blocking the gate.

It's the uncle I stopped calling uncle years ago.

He's drunk. Smiling that smile I grew up dreading. The one that always came before the hurt.

"Look at you," he slurs. "All grown up. Think you can hide from me, little rat?"

I don't answer.

His hand reaches out, filthy, groping.

This time, I don't even think.

I break his jaw with the heel of my palm.

My kicks land harder than I ever thought possible. I hear his ribs break.

There is blood on my shoes. His breath stops before mine does.

I call the police on my phone. I give myself up.

The municipal jail is gray and stinking and rusty.

I sit on the wooden bench, my hands still stained red, my knuckles swollen. The guards don't ask questions.

The woman in a miniskirt across from me in the cell looks at me with a respectful nod and asks if she could braid my hair. I say yes.

I don't tell her my story, but she tells me I remind her of her daughter. The one who left her after losing a battle with dengue. We'd be about the same age now, she says. We even have the same texture hair.

I don't cry, but I let her.

I watch the woman doze off. I slide to the floor and lean against the sticky wall, hoping I could at least rest my burning eyes.

Even then all I think of is the dojo. The lashing rain. Him.

It's dawn when the cell door creaks open.

A young officer gestures for me to stand up and get out. The woman next to me is still fast asleep.

I rise to my feet. My whole body shakes.

I see him standing just outside.

He doesn't even look at me, but I know he's there for me.

The only solid and real thing in my life.

The local police chief is shaking his hand, refers to him as "Mr. Villarete."

We walk out of the station together, across the municipal plaza where his multicab is parked. The sky is gray. The wind bites. The world looks damp and worn.

"Did you put towels by the eastern window?" I ask him suddenly.

He shakes his head. "I forgot."

I sigh. "It's okay. I'll mop it when I get home. I—"

"Cassandra." He never calls me by anything other than my real name. He inhales deeply before continuing. "Are you okay?"

I nod, facing him. My breath clouds between us. My voice cracks as I say, "Why did you come?"

He reaches up.

His hand is warm as it brushes my cheek tenderly, carefully.

"Because you fought back," he says.

That's when I kiss him.

Not out of want. Not at first.

Out of everything else. Pain. Loss. The ashes of stolen girlhood, reborn in his care.

But when he kisses me back, it's like a typhoon unravels inside me. It feels like my sorrow has teeth, and his lips are forgiveness.

We spend the night together, on his mats.

I finally call him by his name, "Anthony."

When I wake up the next morning, he is gone.

The dojo is still there, but it is hollow.

He left no note. No goodbye.

Just…absence.

And the mist of him.

Years later, I stand barefoot in my courtyard.

The gray walls still stand. I repainted them with my own hands.

Children run through the rain-soaked courtyard, laughter ringing off the stone. They swing sticks too big for their arms, shout like they're fighting dragons.

And I let them. Then I will teach them how to be still.

How to breathe. How to rise.

How to rise again after they fall.

I will teach them how to survive without apology.

On my desk, there's a photo. Black and white, grainy with time. It's the only one I have of him.

Eyes like mist. Face like stone. Hands as gentle as the breeze, as strong at the wind.

I trace his face every night. I talk to him often.

But I never saw him again.

But sometimes, when the mist rolls in thick and the ocean before me tastes like salt and promise, I feel him near.

And I smile.

I'll never be alone. I'll never be afraid anymore.

Because I carry him in my bones, in my breath.

In the way I move. In the way I teach.

Because the blood in my veins still remembers the Master that welcomed me home from the mist.

And his kiss that saved me.

CHAPTER 15

The Taste of Her Smile

DON'T THINK SHE KNOWS I EXIST.

But I wait for her.

The kitchen is hot and loud, full of shouting, sizzling, and grease spattering. I stay in the back, quietly, cleaning pots or restocking the line.

I don't have a real chef title, just a name tag and the apron. Just a dream I keep pressed under my tongue.

She walks by the side entrance at exactly 8:47 every week, heels clicking on the concrete, hair tied up in a way that makes her neck look fragile. Her dress always looks expensive. Her smile never quite reaches her eyes.

I watch her through the screen door. The others don't notice her. Or maybe they do, but not the way I see her.

I leave a small container out by the alley gate every Friday night. Always something different. Bone broth when it rains. A *bao* bun with pork and ginger when the wind stings. Fresh mango slices when the air gets heavy and humid. Nothing fancy. Nothing that would be missed.

Sometimes, when I peek after my shift, the container is empty.

Sometimes, she's sitting on the curb with it in her hands, legs tucked under her, heels abandoned beside her.

I don't say anything. I just watch her eat like she hasn't eaten all day.

Once, she left a flower.

A tiny carnation, half-wilted, tucked into the empty bowl.

The following Friday, I added fried rice.

She's not like the others who come to the restaurant—the socialites, the fashion influencers, the girls who take pictures with their food and barely touch it.

She shows up in pageants and fashion shows, sometimes. I see the posters outside the mall. Her name is Mara. She always looks flawless. Perfect cheekbones, large eyes. Painted lips and a graceful posture.

But up close, when she doesn't know I'm looking, she moves like she's about to fall apart.

One Friday, she doesn't show up.

I wait until ten. The food grows cold. My chest feels like it's been scraped out.

The next week, she returns.

She looks paler and thinner. Her collarbones are sharper than I remember. Her lipstick is smudged. She walks slower, hobbling a little on her high heels. That night, I make congee with chicken and egg.

I put it by the alley door.

When I come back for cleanup, she's there.

But this time, she looks up.

"It was you," she says.

Her voice is soft, hollow. She sounds exhausted.

I freeze at the sound, eyes taking in the state of me. My apron is caked with work. My hands are stained with paprika and smell like garlic.

She smiles. Not the smile on her posters, but a real one. The one that looks like it might break.

"Thank you."

I nod.

"I didn't know how to eat anymore," she says quietly. "But you reminded me."

I nod again, and I flee.

After that night, she comes to the restaurant.

Not through the front, never with the other guests. Always the back, through the kitchen. Always the quiet seat near the door, where she can smile at me. My boss lets her in without question.

She doesn't order. She just waits.

And I bring her food.

Chicken *adobo*. *Tortang talong*. Fresh tomatoes and

scrambled eggs over garlic rice. Meals I make in between orders. Meals from home. Meals I remember my mother cooking when I had no appetite.

I ask my boss to deduct the cost from my wages, but Miss Salma says it's okay. She's a fan; maybe Mara will get a title in the next Miss Philippines. She crosses her fingers and grins at me conspiratorially.

Mara always finishes whatever I make for her. She starts to kiss me goodnight, on the cheek. She hugs Miss Salma and thanks her, promising to do her best in the competitions.

And every time she leaves the restaurant through the kitchen door, she looks a little brighter.

One night, I catch her humming as she sits on a step outside the kitchen. The restaurant has a private party inside, but she still chooses to stay.

It's the kind of sound that fills a room, even when it's small. She sounds like she's trying to keep the darkness away.

She hums until her lips start to tremble. Then she stops.

"It's getting harder, Bobby," she tells me. "They want me to be smaller. Thinner. Lighter. I tried. But it hurts now. Everything hurts."

I bring her chicken corn soup. I put it on a stool next to her, so she can reach the bowl easily.

She eats it slowly. Every spoonful to her mouth feels like a prayer.

I don't know how to say the things I want to say. That she doesn't have to disappear to be loved. That food is not the enemy. That she could stay here forever, and I would feed her until the world forgets how to be cruel.

Instead, I say, "I put extra ginger. For your throat. You know, for the question-and-answer portion."

She smiles.

"You always know."

One night, she walks up to me.

It's after close. The kitchen is dim, only the emergency light glowing by the fridge. I'm peeling *kamote* for the sugared fritters she likes, and she's sitting cross-legged on the counter.

Then she steps down quietly. Her head finds my shoulder like it belongs there.

"Don't stop," she says. "Cooking, I mean. Even if I'm not here."

My hands freeze midway.

"You'll always be here," I say, as bravely as I can, smiling through the ripping ache in my chest. "Right?"

She doesn't answer.

Instead she leans in and kisses me.

I kiss her back.

The *kamote* is forgotten.

She takes me up to her apartment, where we make love on her pink-and-white sheets with the red ladybugs.

I don't sleep, but she does. I hold her, and I watch her.

In the morning, I make her breakfast of eggs and toast. I prepare to leave when she gets a reminder that her call time is at ten.

But as she kisses me goodbye, she tells me, "I love you, Bobby."

I put my arms around her and I say it right back.

I leave with the taste of breakfast and her in my heart.

The next Friday, she doesn't come back to the building.

Or the next.

Or the one after.

I wait. I cook. I leave her the *kamote* fritters by the door.

But the container stays full.

I find out from Miss Salma. She calls me into her tiny office, but I know the news before she even says it.

"Mara passed away yesterday," she chokes. "Complications from malnutrition, I think. They said she hid it well. They told me she fought while in the hospital, but her body was too weak."

I don't know what happened next, but I swear the world turned black.

And I heard screaming.

That night, I cook one last meal.

Chicken *adobo*—her absolute favorite. Rice shaped into a heart.

Chicken corn soup and cherry tomatoes for starters. *Kamote* fritters for dessert.

I sit on the step outside the kitchen, the way she used to. I eat in silence. Every bite tastes like goodbye.

When I finish, I close my eyes.

And for just a moment, I feel the weight of her head on my shoulder.

I hear her telling me to not stop cooking.

Like she never left.

Somewhere out there, I think she's smiling.

Somewhere, she's full. Warm and whole.

I keep cooking.

Because someone, somewhere, still needs to eat.

And because love, when it is true, always finds its way to the table.

CHAPTER 16

The Boy at the Bus Terminal

THE FIRST TIME I NOTICE HIM, IT'S RAINING.

I've just stepped off the bus from the city, a duffel slung across my shoulder and my heart heavier than it should be. It's my first month in college. I take the Friday night ride home every week, eyes bleary from exams, ears still ringing with dorm gossip and city noise.

The terminal is quiet at ten in the evening. Most people are already on their way. The light above the waiting bench flickers, the roof leaks, and my umbrella chose this night to give up on me.

He holds out his. A plain black one. No words.

He's maybe my age, or a little bit older. It's hard to tell. He's built lean and tall, hoodie zipped halfway up. His hair is damp, curling just slightly at the ends. His face is unremarkable and unforgettable at the same time.

"You'll get sick," he says softly.

I take it. Not because I'm brave, but because I'm too tired to put up a fight.

"Thanks," I mumble.

He smiles, then fades back into the shadows.

That's how it begins.

Over the months, I learn to look for him.

Sometimes it's Monday morning, when I catch the first bus back to the city before the sun even stretches. Other times, it's Friday nights when I'm too drained to talk to my mother about my week at uni, so I sit awhile, staring at the empty lot behind the terminal.

He's always there. Not always close. Sometimes just a silhouette leaning against a post. Sometimes he's reading. Sometimes he's scribbling something in a notebook.

And always, he somehow knows.

The morning I forget my water bottle, he's already there, unscrewing the cap on a fresh one and handing it to me without a word.

The evening I step on broken glass outside the terminal, barefoot after my sandals snapped, he's there with slippers wrapped in plastic, silently offered.

Another time, he hands me the exact fare for my tricycle ride home when I lose my wallet sometime during the trip from the city.

No matter how unpredictable the week is, he's constant. A strange kind of anchor. A familiar face in a sea of changing ones.

My friends at uni tease me mercilessly.

"You're making up a bus stop boyfriend."

"He sounds like a K-drama plot."

But he's real. To me, he's real.

I ask for his name once.

"I'm Rica," I add.

He takes in the name, and my question.

"Niño," he finally says.

"Means boy," he adds, unnecessarily. "Or child. Take your pick."

"Which one are you?"

"Stuck in between, I think."

"I like it either way," I tell him truthfully. "To me, you're like a vending machine for miracles."

He grins, that lopsided grin that's always a little too soft for someone who never seems to leave the terminal. "Only for you, college girl."

It becomes a rhythm, year in and year out.

It almost feels like some kind of ritual.

I feel safer when he's around. Like the world doesn't stretch quite so far, and I'm not quite so small.

I think he's a student, too, maybe. Or a dropout. Or a dreamer waiting for a bus that never comes.

I don't ask him about these things.

Sometimes I imagine telling him stuff about myself.

Like how my father left us when I was ten, and how I only know him as a name on remittance slips.

How I hate my major, but I'm too scared to switch.

How I sleep with the lights on in the dorm because the dark feels like silence too loud to bear.

But I don't say any of it.

We're not friends. Not really.

But he is…something.

My third year comes.

I start arriving more tired on Fridays and leave more anxious on Mondays. The pressure is on. Papers and the all-consuming thesis. Tests that prepare us for the real-world board exams.

My world starts spinning faster, and I don't get to sit with him as long. He never complains.

"You're growing up," he says, that morning I nearly miss my bus after pulling a Sunday all-nighter to finish my Taxation report.

"Aren't you?"

He smiles, but it doesn't reach his eyes. "I already did."

On my last semester, I come home earlier than usual on a Friday.

The terminal is packed with people coming in from the city. I scan the crowd.

It's graduation next week. I've worked up the guts to ask him if he wanted to come to the city and attend it. Maybe we can even go to the mall after.

He's not there.

For the first time in four years, he's not there.

I sit alone as the crowd thins out, heart thudding.

But then I see it. On the bench.

Our bench.

A folded piece of paper stuck to the back with gum. My name written in his handwriting. I open it with shaking hands.

Congrats, college girl. Keep going. I'll be around.

I come back home after graduation, for a summer internship at the local government office. My mother is very proud that I got *cum laude.*

But for me, it's no more bus rides. No more anxious Mondays or exhausted Fridays.

The next day, I go to the terminal at noon.

It's empty and still. The encroaching heat of summer makes the world feel dried out.

A man in a jumpsuit sweeps the floor near the benches. I ask him casually, like it doesn't matter, like my heart isn't clawing at my ribs.

"Boss, do you know a guy named Niño? He wears a hoodie. Hangs around here a lot."

The man frowns. "You mean the boy who died here?"

I stare at him. "What?"

He leans on his broom. "Hit-and-run. Years ago. Poor kid. Used to go to college in the city. Got stranded one night and decided to walk home. No one saw it happen. But I remember him. He's always respectful. Calls me 'sir.'"

My mouth goes dry. "Do you know his full name?"

"Ah… Niño de Castro, I think. They put up a plaque somewhere. Bus terminal used to hold a candlelight thing every All Souls Day the first few years. But not anymore. People forget."

But I don't.

I never did.

"Thank you, sir," I say to the man. "Thanks for letting me know."

I run off before he sees my tears.

An old clerk at the municipal office tells me there was a boy named Niño de Castro who died almost ten years ago. She was the one who had made arrangements at the funeral home to help out his father. The town officials had pitched in to pay for it.

He'd lived in the next town, a smaller one compared to

ours, where his father had a small farm. He was in his second year at college when the accident happened.

I visit his town. His grave. I bring whatever flowers I can afford.

I sit next to him, on the ground, and cry.

And I tell him everything.

I still go to the bus terminal whenever I can.

I sit on the bench and watch the world go by.

I look at those who are anxious and exhausted, who are happy and excited. They're all there.

But now, I am ready.

I have water, loose change, and an umbrella in my bag. I even have slippers wrapped in plastic, just in case.

Sometimes, someone sits beside me. A freshman. A stranger. Someone lost.

I listen.

And when they leave after saying thanks, I stay.

Just a little while longer.

In case someone needs something.

In case he ever comes back.

In case the last ride never really ends.

ABOUT THE AUTHOR

Shirley Siaton writes edgy and evocative novels and poems. Her worlds are in a deliciously dark cross-section of the romance, neo-noir, action, contemporary, and fantasy genres. Her background in various Asian martial arts inspires a lot of her work.

She has several books of fiction and poetry released since February 2023. Her first book is the free verse collection *Black Cat and other poems*. *Befallen* (March 2025) is her first full-length novel. She also pens juvenile literature as Shirley Parabia.

She is an award-winning writer, poet, and journalist in English, Filipino, and Hiligaynon. Her essays, short stories, and poems have been published internationally in print and digital media. Her multi-lingual plays have been staged in the Philippines.

Shirley is a black belt in Shotokan Karate and an international certified fitness coach. She has a Master's degree in Public Administration and works in education, wellness, and publishing. Originally from Iloilo City, she lives in the Middle East with her husband and two daughters.

ON THE WEB

Shirley's official website:
shirleysiaton.com

Complete reading guide:
shirley.pub

Subscribe to Shirley's VIP list for free exclusive updates:
newsletter.shirleysiaton.com

THE
Silence
BETWEEN
Heartbeats

Love doesn't always stay, but it always leaves something behind . . .

The Silence Between Heartbeats is a collection of sixteen bittersweet stories about love found in fleeting moments—on late-night bus rides, in quiet hotel rooms, across crowded cities, and between strangers who were never quite meant to stay.

Told in whispers and memories, these tales follow people who meet by chance, love without promises, and part with the kind of ache that lingers long after the last word. A ghost who waits at the terminal. A wedding guest who never belonged. An assassin softened by flowers. A boy who cooks love into every dish he will never serve her again.

These are not stories of grand gestures or forever. These are stories of *almosts*, of *if-onlys*, of *one last time*.

And sometimes, that's all love ever needs to be.

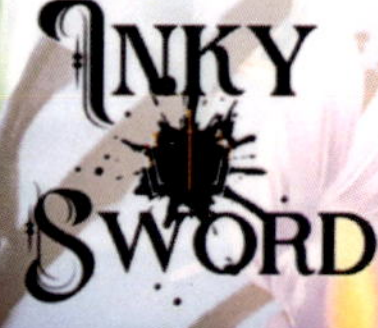

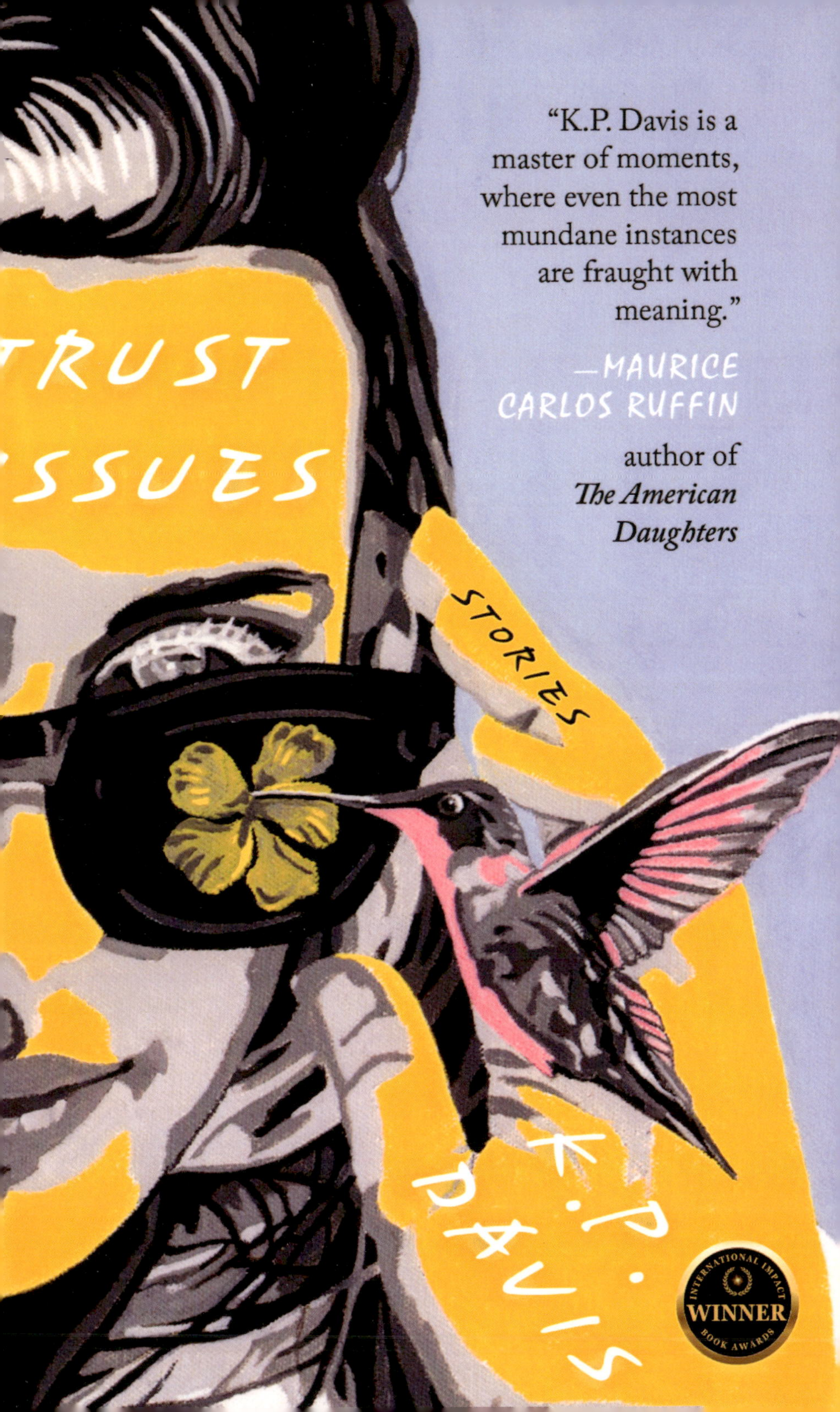

TRUST
ISSUES
STORIES
"K.P. Davis is a master of moments, where even the most mundane instances are fraught with meaning."
—MAURICE CARLOS RUFFIN
author of The American Daughters
K. P. DAVIS
INTERNATIONAL IMPACT BOOK AWARDS
WINNER